The Last Cottage on Pinewood Lane

A Small Town Christmas Romance

MELISSA McCLONE

The Last Cottage on Pinewood Lane
A Small Town Christmas Romance
Copyright © 2022 Melissa McClone
Second Edition

A shorter version of this story was published in
A Keepsake Christmas Anthology.

ALL RIGHT RESERVED

The unauthorized reproduction or distribution of this copyrighted work, in any form by any electronic, mechanical, or other means, is illegal and forbidden, without written permission of the author, except in the case of brief quotations embodied in critical articles and reviews.

This is a work of fiction. Characters, settings, names, and occurrences are products of the author's imagination or used fictitiously and bear no resemblance to any actual person, living or dead, places or settings and/or occurrences. Any incidences of resemblance are purely coincidental.

Cover by Deborah Bradseth at
www.dbcoverdesign.com

Cardinal Press, LLC
December 2022
ISBN-13: 978-1-944777-78-4

Dedication

This one is for me.

Note From Author

A shorter version of this story was published in *A Keepsake Christmas*, an anthology that I participated in with some author friends of mine. The collection was on sale for a few months around the 2021 holiday season. There was a word limit to stories, so I did what I could with that. But I kept thinking of the story and things I would have loved to include or what I might have done a little differently had I been able to expand the word count. So that's what I've done here.

Enjoy,
Melissa

Prologue

Greetings fellow figure skating fans! We here at *Skating Spins & Turns* is your new inside source for all that's happening on and off the ice. Take off your skate guards and get ready while we share all the icy gossip.

From *Skating Spins & Turns*, six and a half years ago:

Pairs champion Natasha "Tasha" Ramson suffered a serious injury during practice. No details have been provided as to what happened, but her longtime partner, Drew Maddox, asked people to send thoughts and prayers for her recovery with the Skate America competition coming up shortly, and he would be sure to make sure she didn't make any evening visits to the hotel bar. We are waiting for a response from Tasha and will update this story as soon as we can.

From *Skating Spins & Turns*, six years ago:

Pairs skater Drew Maddox has a new partner, rising star Kami Procter.

No word on who Tasha Ramson, his former partner, will be pairing up with. Maddox wishes her well and hopes she finds a strong partner who can better handle growth, both in height and weight. We reached out to Tasha for a statement but did not receive a reply from the skater or her representative.

From *Skating Spins & Turns*, five years ago:

Drew Maddox and Kami Proctor have struggled to mesh their styles. Could new partners be on the horizon for both?

Maddox's former partner, Tasha Ramson stood on the podium at her first regional event as a solo skater. Maddox mentioned rumors about elevated scores because of Tasha's mother, Yelena, who is a gold medalist and an influential figure in the skating world. We reached out to the Ramson camp for a statement but did not receive a reply.

From *Skating Spins & Turns*, four years ago:

Drew Maddox and his new partner, Lisbeth Holden,

placed a disappointing sixth at Nationals, but that is a better showing than he had with Kami Proctor, who has retired from the sport.

Tasha Ramson continues to find success as a single skater. But Maddox addressed concerns about Tasha's weight loss. He hopes it isn't like the eating disorder she was prone to as a teenager. We reached out to Tasha for a statement but did not receive a reply from the skater or her representative.

From *Skating Spins & Turns*, three years ago:

Drew Maddox and Lisbeth Holden placed fourth and failed to qualify for the pairs competition at the Winter Games.

US women's champion, Tasha Ramson, came home with two bronze medals from the team event and singles. She then went on to win the World Championships. Her former partner, Drew Maddox, can't believe the improvement in her skating and if he didn't know better, he'd think she was taking PEDs. We reached out to the skating committee and all of none of Tasha's drug tests show any trace of performance enhancing drugs. There was no comment from Tasha or her representative when we asked for a statement.

From *Skating Spins & Turns*, two years ago:

The new pair team to watch this season is Drew Maddox and Savannah Savoy, the only daughter of tech billionaire, Samson Savoy, and his supermodel wife, Siena. We wish them well and hope Maddox can finally find the pair magic he once had with Tasha Ramson.

Speaking of Tasha… She retired after an Ice of Stars Tour and hasn't been heard from sense. Maddox asked that people pray for his partner, who may or may not have a substance abuse problem and be in rehab. No statement was given by Tasha or her representatives when asked about her current situation or whereabouts.

From *Skating Spins & Turns*, one years ago:

Pairs figure skaters Savannah Savoy and Drew Maddox won the national title and will compete at the world championships for the US.

From *Skating Spins & Turns*, three months ago:

Several top skaters, including pairs champions Savannah Savoy and Drew Maddox, who are set to married in an elaborate wedding next spring, will perform in the Nutcracker Holiday Ice show that will make stops in ten cities, starting in November and through mid-December. Winter Games bronze medalist, Tasha Ramson will be an assistant choreographer. Are we the only ones who hope she'll skate in the show?

From *Skating Spins & Turns*, one month ago:

Rehearsals for the first Nutcracker Holiday Ice show in Seattle have begun, but Tasha Ramson was let go as the assistant choreographer after an unknown skater claimed their routine was dangerous and would lead to injury. Drew Maddox asked people to pray that his troubled former pairs partner finds the helps she needs. No statement from Tasha or her representatives was given.

One

December used to be Natasha, aka Tasha, Ramson's favorite time of the year. No longer. The month had barely started but was already turning out to be the worst of her life. And the saddest part? She could do nothing to fix it.

Absolutely nothing.

Tasha stood outside the front door to the Wishing Bay Ice Rink. Her weight shifted between her feet. Right, left, repeat. Except this wasn't one of the figure-skating programs she'd choreographed for one of the rink's skaters. Though if it were, she would call the routine *Impatience*. Not the catchiest title, but all she wanted to do was return inside. Only a few hours remained until the doors closed forever.

A shiver ran through her. A shiver that had nothing to do with the cold temperature in the rink or the slightly warmer one outside. A shiver that had become as familiar as her shadow since hearing her parents had sold the rink.

Keep yourself together.

That was her goal. In a few hours, when she was in her apartment alone, she would allow herself the luxury of falling apart. Until then…

Breathe.

Smile.

Pretend you're okay.

Only one of those tasks appeared doable, but only because of habit, an automatic muscle reflex she couldn't control even if she wanted to. The other two, however, were crucial to getting through the day with as little drama as possible. Yet…

The muscles around her mouth hurt from faking a smile for the past two weeks—when her parents told her and the other employees about the sale of the town's only rink.

Talk about a mic drop.

Mom and Dad hadn't even told her first. She'd heard along with everyone else. Not even Alek had known, or he would have given her a heads up.

The unexpected news sent shock waves through Wishing Bay. Okay, the rink sat on prime real estate. She understood that part. No one would deny its location made developers salivate and had for years. But the sale impacted so many families. Local figure skaters and hockey players would no longer have a nearby rink to practice in. The staff, including Tasha who managed the place, would no longer have jobs. All thanks to her parents' CPA, who advised them to sell. Something about no longer needing the tax write-off and they could invest the money elsewhere. Not that it had ever been a financial investment to them, but a practical one when they moved to the small town on the Washington coast twenty years ago. Now that her brother was a pro hockey player in Seattle, and Tasha was…

Who could blame her for wanting to frown?

She hadn't recovered from the shock and hurt from her parents not bothering to tell her first when she managed the rink. Talk about a slap in the face. Sure, she'd been in Seattle to assist with the choreography at the Nutcracker Holiday Ice show, but that had been a temporary gig. She hadn't realized how short it would turn out to be. She'd still been in charge of the rink operations.

But to be honestly, Mom had pulled stuff like this before. Tasha hadn't thought Dad was capable of something like this, but he'd admitted keeping the news of the sale quiet had been his idea. Somehow, that had hurt Tasha more.

Still, she kept her lips curved upward for appearance's sake. Mom would be on Tasha if she so much as pouted in public. The Ransom name—really Alek's—had to be protected. A good thing the chip on her shoulder was invisible. A chip bigger than the Zamboni she loved to drive and would never get the chance to again.

Don't give up hope.

She didn't want to, but in less than three hours, her life would change. No more paycheck, no more privacy to skate, no more place to go each day after she woke.

Her breath hitched. A tightness in her chest rose to her throat, until her eyes stung.

Stop.

Tasha stared at the overcast, gray sky and blinked. Once, twice, three times. She focused on her breathing until things felt normal again. A lone tear slipped out of her eye. She wiped it away and then blinked until no other tears threatened to fall. Only then did she lower her chin.

Stay calm.

Now wasn't the time to think about the future. Stressing out Mom, who was inside watching the last practice session, would only bring more grief. Tasha also didn't want to worsen her strained relationship with Kristen McAllister, her former best friend and practice partner, who would arrive at any minute for their final exchange of skater costumes.

Don't think about the finality of that, either.

A briny breeze off the bay blew Tasha's hair over her eyes. Her stiff, cold fingers tucked the stray strands under her knit beanie. She shoved her bare hands into her jacket pockets to warm them. She shouldn't have left her gloves inside.

A familiar hatchback zipped into the parking lot like it was auditioning for the next *Fast and Furious* film. The tires squealed to a stop, with the car taking up two spots.

Kristen McAllister had arrived.

Tasha nearly laughed. The haphazard parking job reminded her of taking driver's ed with Kristen, who'd never been a conscientious driver and terrified Tasha whenever she'd sat in the passenger seat. A few things never changed.

Kristen slid out of the driver's seat and grabbed a zippered dress bag with *Wishing Bay Dress Shop* printed across it. Holding on to the hanger sticking out of the bag, she bumped her hip against the door to shut it.

Tasha removed her hands from her pockets. This wouldn't take long, even though they used to spend hours texting and talking. But that was another time and place, when they had believed they would be both best friends and sisters-in-laws.

Suede boots slapped against the asphalt. Kristen wore her blond hair in a messy bun. Not her usual style. Her clothes, too. The yoga pants showed off her long legs and fit physique.

Don't be jealous.

Easier said than done because Kristen's oversized sweatshirt shouldn't seem so fashionable. Tasha had to work harder to look good. Still, those were odd clothing choices. Kristen must not have a shift at her mom's dress shop until later today. Phoebe expected her staff, including her three adult children, to wear business attire or smart casual—emphasis on smart—at the destination boutique.

Working at the rink meant Tasha's clothing choices hadn't changed much over the years. She could easily lace up her skates and be ready to practice on any given day. Kristen no longer skated, but she moved as gracefully as the ice princess she'd once been. She could have been an elite competitor, but Tasha's parents had made Kristen continuing to skate at the rink impossible.

Mom wanted Tasha to be like Kristen, and though Tasha had the skating skills, she was far from princess material. Oh, she hadn't been a frosty villainess or an ugly stepsister. She'd been a workhorse, never giving up when logic suggested she should. And that was probably why Tasha never had a starring role as a gold medal winner of the Ramson family.

Stop thinking.

She plastered on the I'm-doing-great face she'd perfected over the years. And this would be easier compared to other meetings or family dinners. Kristen rarely stayed more than a minute or two.

Kristen came closer. "Sorry I'm late."

She was the same age as Tasha but looked younger

than twenty-eight. Always had, no matter the age. The dark circles around Kristen's eyes, however, weren't normal.

None of my business. Tasha kept her smile frozen in place. She shouldn't care what might be wrong, even though something had to be. Unlike Tasha, Kristen had never been well-acquainted with insomnia. "Not a problem."

Kristen handed over the costume. "Is Giselle practicing?"

"Yes."

"Good, because I don't want to have to deal with her mom." Kristen had dealt with more than one crazy stage mom, but the expression on her face suggested here was more to it this time.

"What happened?" Tasha asked.

"Giselle's costume fits perfectly, but her mom wanted more sparkles, so…"

The casual clothing and tired eyes made sense. "You stayed up all night to add more bling."

"Not all night."

A lie, but only friends called each other on stuff like that. They hadn't been part of each other's lives for eight years other than these quick drop-offs, which had only been occurring for the past three.

Kristen's choice.

Tasha gripped the hanger. The plastic hook dug into her skin. "I appreciate it. Giselle will too. Today's been emotional for her."

"It must be for all of you." Kristen peered around Tasha. "I can't believe your parents sold the rink."

Icy tentacles traveled along Tasha's spine. "Me, neither."

Kristen's inquisitive gaze appeared to be searching for something. "You okay?"

A shrug was the only safe answer. Tasha had gotten good at shrugging—the right shoulder, the left shoulder, both shoulders. Toss in a neutral expression or the hint of a smile, and everyone believed things were fine.

No one wanted the truth—that the sale blindsided Tasha and the rink staff, and she'd been in denial until Mom and Dad told her to pack the office on Black Friday.

This morning, Tasha had awakened with a splitting headache and aching muscles. The pain of hauling boxes reminded her of preparing for Nationals three years ago. She thought she'd never hurt that badly again. She'd been wrong. But this time, the pain wasn't only physical.

Kristen dragged her upper teeth over her bottom lip. "I'm sorry."

Tasha's lips parted, but she struggled with how to respond. Kristen had said those same two words when she no longer wanted to be best friends...or friends at all. The result of the heartbreak caused by Alek, Tasha's twin, when he cut Kristen from his life to focus on his hockey career.

"Thanks." The word came out whisper-soft and almost sounded like a question. But compassion from Kristen McAllister was the last thing Tasha expected. She didn't know how to react.

Kristen rubbed her hands together. That had always been a nervous habit of hers whether before a competition or at school. "The entire town is in shock."

Me too.

But as the daughter of a hall-of-fame hockey player and gold medal figure skater, Tasha had been in the media spotlight her entire life. The spotlight had only intensified when she competed in pairs and then individually. One of her camera-appropriate faces, learned at a young age, had come in handy with the sale. She relied on one now.

Tasha lifted her chin and shrugged slightly again. "The sale was unexpected."

Kristen shoved her free hand into her sweatshirt's front pocket. "Know what you're going to do?"

An invisible band around Tasha's chest tightened, making breathing harder. Her eyelids burned. She blinked.

Do. Not. Cry.

Tears would change nothing, and she didn't need Mom commenting on Tasha's red-rimmed eyes. Nope. She had this.

She schooled her features the way Mom had taught

Tasha when she had to stand on a stepstool to see the bathroom mirror. They'd practiced expressions until the various faces became second nature. She went for nonchalant. It was a tad more approachable, friendly, than the uncommitted one. "No idea."

Kristen's gaze sharpened. "You must hate not knowing."

Tasha cleared her dry throat. Her voice was harder to control when she got emotional. "I do."

"This might be a blessing in disguise. You're too talented for a run-down, twenty-year-old rink. You could coach or choreograph or do something outside of skating."

Even though Mom and Dad told the staff they sold the rink on advice from their accountant, they also believed working at the rink kept Tasha from reaching her true potential. She'd been too afraid to ask if she'd been a reason for the sale. Afraid her getting too comfortable had cost Wishing Bay its ice rink. "Skating is all I know."

Kristen started to speak but then pressed her lips together.

"What?" Tasha asked.

"Nothing."

Tasha half laughed. They might not be friends, but she remembered Kristen's tells as if nothing had changed. "That's not true."

Kristen exhaled slowly. "Skating hasn't been kind to you."

"No, it hasn't."

But the entire ice world and anyone who followed figure skating knew that. Unfortunately, the hits kept coming, but Tasha hadn't thought her parents would be the ones firing her this time. In hindsight, she shouldn't have been surprised. They were just two more in a long line that included Kristen.

Heat rushed through Tasha's body. "That's why I've spent the last three years managing this ice rink. But you haven't been kind to me, either."

There.

Tasha had finally said it. Something she'd wanted to say for years. It wasn't the day to go all-in with her emotions, but too late. And the weight she'd carried for far too long lifted, floating away like grains of sand in the wind.

Kristen's features hardened into a frown. "I had my reasons."

Ones that had nothing to do with Tasha and everything to do with Alek, Mom, and Dad. Yet, she'd been the one to pay the price. "Your reasons didn't make it any easier on me."

Though she didn't expect an apology, Tasha found herself wanting one. Too much time had passed, however, and it turned out Alek had made the correct decision for his career by closing the door on his friendship with Kristen, his high school sweetheart.

Maybe Tasha should do the same, given nothing

would be the same after the rink's doors closed for the last time today. She had no reason to remain in Wishing Bay or to stay in touch with anyone beyond a text on birthdays or Christmas. Even then, that might be unnecessary.

Kristen rubbed the back of her neck. "I heard your narcissist ex-skating partner got you fired as the assistant choreographer for the Nutcracker Holiday Ice show in Seattle."

Subject change, but Tasha had said what she needed to.

"Rumor, but it's most likely true." On the twenty-fifth, if anyone was keeping track. The date had been burned on her heart, one more reminder to stay away from the guy. Drew Maddox had disappointed her or broken her heart more times than she cared to remember. But she'd never imagined he wanted to destroy her, especially after so long. They'd broken up more than six years ago. "You told me to watch out for him way back when. I should have listened."

But the attention of the older, handsome skater who wanted to be Tasha's partner on and off the ice had filled a need to belong she still couldn't fully explain. Except everything she'd thought about him had been wrong. He hadn't filled a thing. Instead, he'd taken everything she had to give. Everything she'd once been.

It was Kristen's turn to shrug. "Some lessons have to be learned the hard way."

"I learned them." And boy, talk about hard.

"I should probably—"

"Not yet." Tasha didn't want the conversation to end, but she needed to be there when the skaters left the ice at the end of the practice session. "You're welcome to have one last look around. It's part of your history, too."

Kristen's eyes widened. "Are they tearing down the rink?"

"A complete remodel. At least that's what the new owners claim."

"You don't believe them?"

"Wishing Bay is becoming more popular with tourists. This property is prime real estate. The buyers might have said anything to get their offer accepted."

Kristen's lips slanted. "You never used to be this cynical."

"Not cynical. Realistic." Tasha was getting colder. "Come in for old times' sake. It'll only take a minute."

Kristen took a step forward. "Wait. Are your parents here?"

"My mom is."

"No, thanks." The words flew out like a puck off a stick during a shootout. "I need to go."

Kristen hated Tasha's parents, who'd convinced Alek he had no room in his life or heart for anything but hockey.

"Still avoiding my mom?" Tasha asked.

"Your dad and Alek too. Eight years and counting, but I travel so much for the dress shop avoiding them around town hasn't been a problem."

Tasha hadn't realized Kirsten had done that on purpose. The words "I'm sorry" sat perched on the tip of her tongue. She she'd done nothing wrong, so she remained silent.

Kristen pulled her hand out of her pocket. Her keys rattled against each other in her right hand. "Good luck wherever you land."

Wherever was the key word. "Thanks."

"Have a merry Christmas."

"You, too." Which went without saying because Phoebe McAllister would never let her three adult children have a bad holiday. "I'm hoping my Christmas won't be a blue one."

"Doing something special?"

"Going to Berry Lake."

Kristen's nose crinkled. "Where's that?"

"Near Mount Adams." Tasha recalled the photographs of the quaint storefronts and lake Serena Tremblay, and a successful life coach and the wife of Alek's teammate Logan, had called her hometown a wonderful place to spend the holidays. "It's a small town someone said I should visit."

Kristen laughed. The sound still made Tasha smile. "You've always wanted a Hallmark movie kind of holiday."

Tasha flinched. "I'm surprised you remembered."

"Every December, you complained about build snowmen from sand, not snow."

"I still do even though I've enjoyed the coastal Christmases spent here. But there's no reason to spend the holidays in Wishing Bay this year, so now I can check off a white Christmas from the bucket list."

"How long will you be there?"

"Until December thirty-first."

"That long?"

The stay, a gift from Alek after Tasha expressed interest in going there, was going to be shorter. But Kristen didn't need to know that. "When I found out the rink was closing, I extended my stay."

"Is your…um…family going with you?"

"Nope. Mom and Dad will be in Seattle." *With Alek* remained unspoken.

Kristen smirked. "Your mom must hate that."

"She's furious." Tasha laughed again. The unexpected sound loosened the knots, tied tighter than skate laces, in her stomach. "I gave her presents to take with them to Seattle, but she's still trying to convince me not to go."

"It's not like you haven't spent holidays away from them before. Don't let your mom change your mind.

Tasha drew back. "You sound like you mean that."

"I do." Uncomfortable silence stretched between them—a reminder that they were no longer part of each other's lives and futures. "Well, drive safe. And have fun with your Hallmark Christmas."

Fun wasn't on the agenda, but no one needed to know that. "Enjoy yours."

Tasha planned to skip the holiday this year. That would be easy to do in Berry Lake where no one knew her. She would forget about Christmas, her family, and the rink. Her only task would be to figure out what to do next, even though none of her plans had ever worked out.

But there was always a first time, right?

Somewhere out there was a place she belonged. All she had to do was find it.

Two

Elias Carpenter slumped behind his desk at his family's law office in Berry Lake, Washington. Twenty-nine was too young to hate his job this much. He enjoyed being a lawyer. What he didn't like was still being treated like a first-year intern after working there for more than five years. The future he'd once dreamed about looked...not bleak—he owned a nice house near the lake and a top-of-the-line SUV—but...exhausting.

Something had to give. He didn't want it to be him.

The sun had set three hours ago, leaving nothing but darkness outside his window. His hands itched to grab his suit jacket and overcoat, and his feet wanted him to stop being so responsible and bolt out of there.

Forget about bringing his laptop with him. He would leave it behind and pretend he wasn't his firm's lowly lawyer for a night.

A nice fantasy, except...

If he didn't work late, he would end up there tomorrow night and likely the entire weekend…again.

Be careful what you wish for.

A cliché, yes. But one hundred percent the truth when Gramps and Dad controlled Elias's livelihood—controlled him.

Ignoring the four walls closing in on him, Elias pushed aside the file and reached for the Advent calendar his grandmother had given to him. He opened the door—not even paying attention to the number on it—removed the piece of chocolate shaped like a present, complete with a bow, and popped the candy into his mouth.

The smooth flavors melted on his tongue.

Delicious.

Leave it to Grammy to splurge on a more expensive box of candy. For as long as he remembered, she gave him a calendar on Black Friday to open throughout December. He enjoyed doing that as an adult as much as he had at age ten. But he would forgo the other twenty-four chocolates if it would make time speed up or warp, so tomorrow when he woke, it would be January first.

Elias didn't hate Christmas. He enjoyed singing carols, drinking Grammy's hangover-guaranteed eggnog, and opening presents on Christmas morning. But given the way Dad and Gramps kept piling work on him, by the time the twenty-fifth rolled around,

Elias would be a modern-day Bob Cratchit, begging his two familial Scrooges for the day off.

Of course, none of the extra cases were interesting, only ones they deemed unworthy of their legal expertise, experience, and time. It always came down to time. Theirs being more valuable than his.

A groan—unnatural, raw, unrefined—ripped from his throat. Not the way a representative from a respected law firm should sound. At least that was what Dad would say—more like lecture. For once, Elias didn't care. Maybe he should embrace this secret side of himself that no one else knew and go public by entering the Sasquatch-calling contest at next summer's Bigfoot Seekers Gathering.

If he lasted that long.

Grammy claimed Christmas wishes were real, but Elias didn't know what to wish for—a new job, a new attitude, a new life. Honestly, anything other than another new tie would be an improvement over the status quo.

Stuck in Berry Lake.

The words might as well be lyrics from a melancholy country song. His hometown had a 24/7 rumor mill, a dive bar with a PhD-holding bartender, and more drama than a four-digit population should have, so it wouldn't be much of a stretch.

Elias rolled his head to one side and then the other, stretching his stiff neck muscles. He'd sat for too long, but the movement didn't help.

The pain between his eyebrows sharpened.

It wasn't yesterday's jackhammer intensity, where only darkness and extra-strength painkillers provided relief. This ache was more like a drunk woodpecker whose beak occasionally hit its mark.

Go home.

He should. A guy with a life would be at his kitchen table with a beer, a plate of home-cooked food, and someone sitting next to him. Someone with a pretty smile, eyes only for him, and who smelled nice.

Not that he'd gone out on a date in weeks. Or had it been months?

Elias couldn't remember. Talk about the sad cherry on the top of his nonexistent personal life.

His headache intensified.

Uh-oh. The woodpecker appeared to be sobering up.

Focus. He had work to do.

A knock, and then his door opened. Dad, aka Marc Carpenter, Junior to friends and clients, stepped in and left the door open. "Hard at work, as usual."

"You and Gramps keep passing on cases to me."

Shoulders back and chin lifted, Dad stood like Zeus on Mount Olympus about to throw a lightning bolt over the desk. "That's the price you have to pay to move up in the firm."

Elias's shoulders bunched, and his neck got even stiffer. Dad and Gramps called the soul-crushing workload paying one's dues. In the beginning, sure. But Elias was no longer fresh from law school. Dad occasionally called him a partner in front of clients, but when they were alone, Elias was nothing more than the firm's worker bee. The pay was good, but money no longer held the same appeal as say…happiness.

"What do you need now?" Elias's resigned tone brought a cringe. *Ugh.* He didn't want to turn into a whiny complainer, but fighting the bone-weary exhaustion was…well, exhausting.

He'd once eyed his luxurious office filled with leather wingback chairs, mahogany cabinets, bookcases, and desk with pride. Now, the room was nothing more than a well-appointed prison cell.

Dad's lips slanted into a thin, disapproving line. That only happened on the rare occasions Elias failed to do as told with no questions asked. "You must represent the law firm on the Winter Extravaganza committee."

Must.

No question mark at the end.

Not even a *please.*

Again, typical.

Bob Cratchit had survived until Christmas. Elias might not. He eyed the Advent calendar. Doors two to seven looked mighty tempting.

"The proceeds benefit local nonprofits," Dad added as if not everyone in town had been talking about the fundraiser.

Well, everyone at Brew and Steep. The coffee shop on his way to work had been the only place Elias visited this week.

"I know what the Extravaganza is, but I don't have time to volunteer." The pile of work might as well be sitting on top of his chest. Breathing took more effort. "Besides, Gramps and Grammy are on it. Grammy told me they attended a few meetings before Thanksgiving."

Something flashed on Dad's face. Not panic, more like concern. Dad drove him hard, but despite Elias's complaints tonight, Dad was a good guy. Better than most other fathers in town. But worry wasn't an emotion often displayed toward Elias, because he never gave him a reason to worry. That suggested this involved someone else. Most likely his grandparents.

Elias had loosened his tie thirty minutes ago, but his collar tightened. He forced himself not to tug at it or unbutton the top. Show no weakness had been ingrained in him at a young age. "Is something wrong?"

"Not wrong." Dad licked his lips, an unfamiliar gesture that made Elias hold his breath. "Your grandmother had a doctor's appointment today to review test results. There's…an issue."

Elias's breathing stilled. His pulse launched into the stratosphere. Forget Elmer's glue. Grammy was Gorilla Glue personified. She held the Carpenter family together. Without her…

His knee bounced. He lifted off his chair. He wanted to demand answers and the doctor's number. Not that the doc would tell him anything because of HIPAA.

He forced himself to sit. "Tell me what's going on."

Dad inhaled slowly. His exhale came even slower.

An imaginary clock in Elias's head got louder. *Tick-tock. Tick-tock. Tick-tock.* "Tell me."

"It's. Her. Heart." Dad drew out the words so long each word sounded like its own sentence.

Her heart.

Worst-case scenarios flashed through Elias's brain at fast-forward speed. Grammy in a hospital bed attached to blinking and beeping machines. A flatline on a heart monitor. A coffin surrounded by the fragrant lilies she loved so much.

"Three weeks ago, she was given a heart monitor to wear. Now, she needs a pacemaker," Dad said as if Grammy was ordering a purse to match a new pair of shoes.

Elias was about to say as much, but he remembered the lip lick. This had to be bothering Dad, but the man had built a reputation of being calm and capable and strong, a rock for the family and the community. If that meant shutting off emotions to be a solid pillar no matter the circumstances, Marc Carpenter didn't think twice. That was why Elias closed his eyes, took a breath, and opened them.

Except, Dad's stop-being-so-dramatic expression he reserved for Elias's mom's shopaholic tendencies was fully displayed. "The procedure is routine. Simple."

"We're talking about her heart." Elias's voice sounded surprisingly steady, though it wavered slightly at the end. He usually kept his cool, but this was Grammy they were talking about. She was his Achilles' heel. The closest thing to a mother figure he had. After his parents divorced, his mother had gone no contact with Elias. "Grammy is seventy-nine. Any procedure at her age carries risks."

But Grammy would be fine. She had to be.

Wait. Dad had mentioned something about three weeks…

Elias balled his hands. His temperature shot from ninety-eight point six to two hundred twelve. "Why didn't anyone tell me what was going on?"

"You didn't need to know." The sharpness of Dad's words stabbed like a knife. "Now, you do."

More proof they saw him as a teenager, not a grown man. "What changed?"

"Your grandfather and I want her to slow down. She won't if Gramps doesn't. I'm too busy to be on the committee."

Which meant Elias had no choice but to do it.

An image of an office in a high-rise in Seattle or Portland flitted through his mind. Who was he kidding? A low-paying job as a public defender might be better than languishing in quicksand daily at his family's firm. A new job would mean leaving Grammy, but if he stayed, he would work himself to death for the firm.

He swallowed back regret at having become nothing more than the firm's lackey. Grammy loved him, but Gramps and Dad only seemed to care about him if Elias did what they wanted. How would they act if he said no to their demands? He didn't know because he'd always said yes, though that was getting harder to do. "What's involved with the committee?"

Dad shuffled through the stack of files. "Attend the next meeting. Do whatever task you're assigned."

Elias wanted to help Grammy, but "task" was too vague. He leaned back in his chair to exude more confidence and pointed to the files. "I have a huge workload thanks to you and Gramps."

His dad scoffed, slapping the files against the desk and sending the stack to the floor. With a contrite expression, he stepped away from the desk.

Of course, Dad didn't clean up his mess. That was Elias's job. He bent to pick up the files and placed them on the desk.

"You're young." Dad sounded wistful—a rarity for such a pragmatic man. "You can handle the lack of sleep. And don't forget, one day, all this will be yours."

"Be more specific about one day?"

Dad laughed. "Want to get rid of us?"

Yes, which meant Elias needed to answer carefully.

On paper, returning to his hometown after law school checked all the boxes on his life plan. A position at his family's thriving firm—albeit in a small town— gave him job security and a future with a location close to loved ones. Except Elias never expected to be stuck in the role of a glorified intern.

Forget about the treatment getting old. It was beyond black-squishy-banana-drawing-fruit-flies rotten. "Gramps could've retired ten years ago but he comes into the office every day."

"He enjoyed the accolades when a case goes well."

Which they did because of Elias. Even Dad relished the credit for work Elias did. Both of the elder Carpenter men loved being seen as the "big fish" in Berry Lake.

Which meant Elias shouldn't expect them to treat him differently once he turned thirty or forty. Possibly even fifty.

The knot in his gut quadrupled. He'd followed the rules, kept his thoughts to himself, and worked hard. Look where that had gotten him. Even though he always wore a life jacket, he wasn't one to rock the boat, but the oars had disappeared, and water was filling the hull. Sometimes capsizing was the only—the best— option.

"We need to hire more staff." The words rushed out like the snowmelt feeding into Berry Lake. "There's too much for one lawyer."

The deep lines on Dad's face would draw the rock climbers to town better than the local crags. "Three attorneys work here."

Elias laughed, deep from his belly. The sound rumbled through him and loosened the knots inside him. That only appeared to irk Dad more. Elias wasn't about to stop. He couldn't.

He pushed the re-staked files toward Dad. "Take your cases back. I can't do all this extra work if I have to be on some stupid committee."

"What's wrong with you?" Dad's furrowed brow matched the confusion in his voice. "The Extravaganza will be excellent publicity for the firm."

Seriously? Elias glanced around his office as if expecting to see a hidden camera or a film crew pulling a prank. "We're the only lawyers in town."

"It's called giving back." His father's face turned a festive holiday red. "Do you have any idea how lucky you are? How many lawyers would appreciate the opportunity we've given you?"

"No." Elias's law school classmates hadn't been impressed by his interning at his family's law office. While friends gained prestigious law clerk positions, he hadn't even applied. "How many?"

Dad's eyebrows drew even closer until they nearly met. "What's gotten into you?"

"I'm tired."

Elias didn't want to argue. Helping Grammy was

his priority, but he needed more in his life than doing work that went unappreciated and left him unfulfilled. A new job would have to wait until Grammy felt better.

He rubbed his gritty eyes. "Anything I should know about being on the committee?"

Dad's posture relaxed. "We're an official sponsor, so don't offer to pay for anything more."

Not a surprise. Dad focused on the bottom line more than Gramps did. But if Elias quit, the firm wouldn't survive without a massive reorganization and new hires.

"Keep your grandmother looped in, so she doesn't feel left out. Oh, and she mentioned something about Sabine Culpepper's animal rescue foster program happening in conjunction with the benefit, so you may find yourself involved with that too."

Animal foster?

Before Elias could formulate a sentence, Dad headed out of the office. Then, he stopped at the doorway and faced Elias. "It's clear the Extravaganza isn't something you want to take on, but it'll help your grandparents."

Elias's gaze bounced from Dad's empty hands to the files stacked on the desk, still sitting at the same high level. "I said I'll do it. But talk to Gramps about hiring an associate and a paralegal at minimum."

Dad's lips thinned. "We'll see."

Better than a straight-out no, but it wasn't enough.

Elias wanted to help people so justice was served. He took pride in representing Missy Hanford, accused of setting the Berry Lake Cupcake Shop on fire, but those cases rarely ended up on his desk. Jenny Hanford O'Rourke was only reason he was Missy's attorney. He hated that she was accused of arson, but he was grateful for the opportunity to prove her innocence and himself. One more neighborly dispute and he might lose it for good.

January.

He would have to wait until then.

But come the new year, if Dad and Gramps didn't hire additional staff, Elias would revise his life plan so it no longer involved the family firm…

Or Berry Lake.

Elias hoped Grammy would understand.

Three

Tasha should have left an hour ago, yet she remained in the eerily empty rink. Everyone else had gone home. Oh, she'd been there with no skaters every day, but this was the last time, and her heart bled as if sliced open by a newly sharpened blade.

Enjoy it while you can.

She slowly inspected the interior to make sure nothing had been forgotten. Each crack in the wall or tear in the carpet or ding in a locker brought back a memory, sometimes more. The ache in her heart intensified, each beat of it bringing the final goodbye that much closer.

Tasha stared at the bench where she'd sprained her ankle dancing when she should have been warming up, passed by the spot where Alek's bloody nose stained the carpet, and touched the rail where she'd been kissed for the first time by Robbie Davis on a dare. She ran her palm against the rail. "Thank you."

For the good times. And the bad times.

The rink had been a home away from home for much of her life. No one would ever know she'd slept in the office last night. A final hurrah so to speak that included a midnight skate with the music blasting.

Mom's signature fragrance announced her arrival before her footsteps did. Yelena, an expensive perfume, was named after her and sold in a gold bottle to match the medal she'd won for Russia competing with the Unified team in figure skating nearly thirty years ago.

"I went through the office and snack bar. Your father wants me to pick up dinner on my way home, so it's time to go." Mom's designer clothing and glowing skin made her look to be in her late thirties, not her early fifties. But her nonchalant tone bristled.

She tsked. "Don't pout."

Mom claimed showing extreme emotions caused wrinkles, but Tasha didn't care. She gripped the railing like a lifeline. "A few minutes saying goodbye won't hurt me."

Mom scoffed. "You've been moping around for the past two weeks. And for what? You deserve better than working yourself ragged at this rink."

"You keep saying that."

"Is true." Even though Mom had lived in the US

for twenty-nine years, she still had an accent and spoke Russian whenever she could.

"I love this place." Her parents had built the rink not as a business investment, but so their family could skate without driving an hour and a half away. The ice rink had been more than a place to practice. It kept Tasha from drowning each time her life imploded, which happened even after she'd retired thanks to her former pairs partner vicious lies. "I thought you did too."

"It served its purpose."

"For you, maybe."

Mom sighed, a long exhale rivaling the wind that often whipped off the bay. "You are meant for more."

"What if I don't want more?" *Oops.* Tasha hadn't meant to be that open...honest.

"Alek—"

"We may be twins, but we're not the same." Not even close. Despite training until her body revolted, she'd had to settle for tarnished bronze. Unlike her brother and parents' gold medal legacy. Her World Champion gold didn't even count toward the Winter Game tally. "This rink has been everything to me. Even if the new owners ask me to stay on, the renovations will take months."

Mom sniffed. "Could use a remodel."

The worn, stained carpet, dingy gray walls, old and dated fixtures needed replacing, but...

What about me?

Tasha bit the inside of her cheek. The metallic taste of blood hit her tongue.

"You've been hiding here." Mom's accent became more pronounced, a sign she was losing patience. "Is time to move on from the past and live in the present."

Talk about a toe pick to the forehead.

Tasha's hands balled. Couldn't Mom show some compassion? Unfortunately, that wasn't Yelena Ramson's style. Mom had earned the nickname Ice Queen for being unflappable in competitions and never showing emotion beyond what the choreography demanded. Strange, when Dad wore his emotions like a favorite T-shirt for all to see. "Mom—"

"You're a survivor. You'll survive this."

"Of course, I will. I've survived worse." Tasha's voice came out stronger—more confident—than she felt. "I'm also twenty-eight. Old enough to decide how to live."

Or when to hide.

Mom's expression was not unsympathetic, but her competitive streak ruled. She didn't want to win. She *needed* to win. No matter what it took or who paid the price. Dad and Alek were the same. Tasha used to be, too, until she realized others had more control of her destiny than she did.

Mom stepped closer, close enough for a hug, which Tasha desperately needed, but Mom's arms remained pressed by her sides. "Then change your mind and come to Seattle with us for Christmas."

Forget Tasha's uncertain future. Mom only wanted her family together over the holiday. And not to have them all together for the family time. No, Alek got a couple days off for Christmas, and Mom wanted to take advantage of the time for photo ops. "My vacation is fully paid for. The money is nonrefundable."

Not that Alek cared about the money. But he knew Tasha needed to get away. And she did.

"We'll pay—"

"I'm not canceling." Tasha raised her chin. "A vacation in a winter wonderland is what I need."

Mom's gaze softened. She touched Tasha's shoulder, and Tasha leaned into it more than she should, but Mom didn't show this kind of emotion often. This counted as an almost-hug, right? Mom's mouth lifted in a Mona Lisa smile, but it was the affection in her eyes that brought a lump to Tasha's throat, and she fought the temptation to lean in closer.

Mom kissed her head. "You need more than that, *moya solnishka.*"

Tasha's heart skipped a beat—possibly three. Wishing Bay was at sea level, but her struggle to breathe reminded her of high-altitude training. She loved the kinder, gentler Yelena the press and public saw.

As Mom lowered her hand, Tasha nearly fell sideways. She caught her balance and straightened.

"Maybe I'll find what I'm looking for in Berry Lake."

"When do you leave?"

"Saturday."

Mom's lips parted, but no words came out. That was unlike her. "Remember, Natasha. You are in control of your destiny."

Softness gave way to strength in Mom's eyes and voice—the same kind of strength Tasha would need to get through the rest of the year, possibly longer.

"You can't keep spinning, hoping when you stop, everything will be okay," Mom added.

Tasha half laughed. "Don't worry. I stopped spinning a long time ago."

She didn't want to do that again and repeat her past.

She couldn't.

* * *

Saturday afternoon, Elias stood on his front porch. The cold air bit like tiny fangs on his face and hands, and the below-freezing temperature chilled him to the bone. He shivered, wishing he'd put on a coat before answering the door, but how was he supposed to know Sabine Culpepper's visit wouldn't be a drop-and-dash?

Right about now, he should wake from the nightmare. The best part was not working on a weekend, which suggested he was dreaming. Except the small mangy brown and white dog attached to the other end of the leash he held was real. And the number of items piling up on his porch like someone had gone on a Cyber Monday shopping spree kept piling up.

He flexed his cold fingers. "Does a dog need this much…stuff?"

Sabine placed another box on top of a black wire cage. She adjusted the down vest she wore over the Berry Lake Animal Rescue sweatshirt. "We provide our Home for Holidays fosters with all the supplies they need. You'll find an instruction sheet and numbers to call if you need help with your temporary family member. I will warn you since you're new to this, a few people have earned the term foster failures."

Elias cringed. Her gleeful tone sounded more like a plaintiff winning a six-figure settlement than an animal rescuer. "I hope they didn't hurt any animals."

Sabine's face lit up. "Nope. They adopted them. Foster failure, get it?"

Elias did, but he wasn't worried. He'd been roped into fostering, but it wouldn't go further than that. "Fostering for my grandmother was mentioned but nothing about adoption. I won't be failing at this."

Sabine winked. "That's what they all say."

The odds of an asteroid hitting the Earth or buying a winning lottery ticket would be better than him adopting anything, including a goldfish. Come

December twenty-sixth, the dog would return to the rescue with all its stuff. He didn't have time for a personal life, let alone a pet. Elias eyed one item warily. He didn't want to keep the dog, he didn't want it locked up as if this were a zoo, which begged the question. "Why did you bring a cage?"

"It's a dog crate." Sabine's patient tone suggested she might have heard his question before. "Many dogs feel safe and comfortable in them when they're alone during the day or when they sleep at night. This crate came to the rescue with Higgins, so it's familiar."

"Her name is Higgins?" Elias asked.

Sabine tilted her head. "His name is Higgins."

A *boy dog, right*. He should remember that.

But what kind of name was Higgins? It sounded like a butler with a stiff upper lip and a stuffy British accent. "Is that his real name?"

"It is. We know Higgins's history, which isn't often the case." Sabine petted the dog, whose tail wagged like a broken metronome. "A car hit his person. He was killed instantly."

"Tragic."

"This little one was alone for a night until someone remembered about him."

Poor guy. Elias hoped Higgins hadn't been scared. Wait. Did dogs get scared? Still… "That's sad."

Nodding, Sabine rubbed behind the dog's ear. "The man had no will."

Elias's temperature shot up lightning quick. He gripped the leash tighter.

"What's wrong with people? They can download a fill-in-the-blank will off the internet. If you have a dependent…" He blew out a breath, trying to gain control of himself, but this was a massive pet peeve. "Sorry. Occupational hazard."

"Right there with you, but few people think they're going to die." Sabine patted the dog's head before standing straight. "The man's parents surrendered the dog. After a few transfers from overcrowded shelters, Higgins ended up at ours. You're lucky. He's super smart and chill."

Elias pictured his newly installed wide-planked hardwood floors. "Potty trained?"

"He's had no accidents at the shelter or in the van."

Elias's bunched shoulders relaxed slightly. Maybe this wouldn't be so bad.

Sabine eyed him warily. "You're up for fostering, right?"

Nope. He forced a smile.

"Of course." He used his trial voice, which worked miracles with jurors whenever he was allowed in the courtroom. "It's one more way to support the Extravaganza and your rescue."

"You're doing a great job at the temporary ice rink."

"Thanks." Overseeing the rink's installation in the

town's park had been easy, which explained why he'd volunteered for that job. He just needed to stop by each day to make sure the volunteers were doing what they'd signed up to do.

"You took your grandparents' place on the committee," Sabine said. "Were you talked you into fostering?"

"No." He didn't hesitate because that was one hundred percent the truth. It hadn't been his grandparents but his father. However, Dad might not be thrilled when Elias had to go home at lunchtime to let the dog out and could no longer stay late. Fostering might work out better than he imagined. "Don't worry. I've got this."

Elias sounded so confident he'd almost convinced himself.

Sabine bit her lip.

He didn't want her to cross-examine him. "Don't you have other animals to drop off?"

"I do, but—"

"Higgins and I will be fine."

"Okay." Sabine headed to her van and opened the door. She faced him. "Have fun."

Fun might be pushing it. Still, Elias would make the best of the situation for the law firm's reputation and the orphaned dog. He glanced at the closest box. A stocking with *Higgins* written in glitter glue across the cuff sat on top.

"Guess we should hang your stocking next to mine."

Higgins panted.

As Sabine drove away, Elias waved. He carried a bag and box and led the dog into the house. He set the items on the floor before taking the dog away from the door. "Stay here while I bring in the other items."

Higgins sat, and his tail wagged.

The tension in Elias's muscles eased. "Good boy."

Elias brought in the rest of the bags and boxes. Higgins hadn't moved. "Sabine's right. You're a smart dog."

As if on cue, Higgins tilted his head. Big brown eyes stared up at Elias.

Something unfamiliar and unwelcome shifted in his chest. He rubbed over his heart. "Stop it right now."

The dog's head slanted more, and the tail wagging stopped.

"Nope. It won't work." Elias pointed at Higgins. "I'm telling you. I won't be one of those foster failures. Your being here is temporary. T-E-M-P-O-R-A-R-Y."

Not that even intelligent dogs could spell.

Higgins's expression didn't change.

Elias fought the urge to roll his eyes or comfort the dog. The battle was real. "Did she train you to do those puppy dog eyes so fosters fall in love with you?"

Unsurprisingly, Higgins didn't answer.

No matter. "I have a job. A life. It's not fair to leave you alone all day, even though Sabine said you were used to the cage…crate. And sorry your, um, person died, and you ended up with me."

Higgins's sad expression made Elias want to pick the dog up, but he wasn't the cuddling type. Best to leave the dog to get acclimated. "The only thing left outside is the crate. Stay there."

Once again, the dog didn't move. Sabine was correct about the dog being chill too.

Elias left the front door cracked to make it easier to open. Outside, he picked up the crate. It was lighter than he expected but bulky. He maneuvered his way inside and placed the crate against a wall in the living room. That would be a suitable spot for it.

His phone rang.

Of course, his phone was on the coffee table.

Elias left the door open and grabbed his phone. Grammy's name flashed on the screen. He accepted the call. "Hey, Grammy. How are you feeling?"

"I'm fine. Your grandfather is being a worrywart."

"He loves you."

"He just doesn't want to have to find a new wife," Grammy teased. "Are things going well with the Extravaganza?"

"Yes, but the committee is still debating this year's Christmas performance."

"Let me guess. Penelope Jones and Charlene Culpepper can't agree."

Of course, Grammy would know what was happening even if she wasn't involved personally. "You nailed it."

She sighed. "I'm sorry you had to take my place."

So was Elias, but he would never admit that to Grammy. "It's not so bad. The Berry Lake Cupcake Shop provides dessert and Brew and Steep brings coffee."

"That's the spirit." Grammy's enthusiasm filled Elias with warmth. "Did Sabine drop off the foster dog?"

Elias gripped the phone. "About fifteen minutes ago."

"Tell me about the dog."

"His name is Higgins, and he's potty trained. Sabine said he's chill."

The clicking of paws made Elias look over at Higgins. A blur of blue headed out the front door. His stomach dropped. "Grammy, I need to go."

"Talk to you later, dear. I love you."

He disconnected from the call. "Dog. Higgins. Stop."

Pulse pounding, Elias raced out the door. His feet sank into the snow covering his front yard.

Higgins ran toward the end of Pinewood Lane. The blue leash dragged behind him like a malfunctioning kite tail.

The dog wouldn't get far. Elias's legs and strides would overtake the dog's shorter legs soon.

His breath huffed. At least no cars. "Higgins!"

The dog didn't slow but sped up.

So much for Higgins being smart and chill. The dog needed obedience lessons.

Or a new foster.

Elias picked up the pace, ignoring the stitch in his side and the burn in his thighs. He'd been away from the gym for too long if a brief run wore him out.

Higgins ran past the last cottage. He veered between the tall pine trees onto the path that led to the frozen lake. For a dog who'd only arrived, he seemed to know where he wanted to go.

Please don't go on the ice.

It would be harder to catch the dog out there.

"Higgins." Elias's voice hung on the wind.

He cleared the trees to a snow-covered area known as Pinewood Beach in the summer. Higgins sat facing the lake at the edge, where a short ridge of snow had built up. He walked slowly so as not to spook the dog.

Movement caught Elias's attention. He glanced past Higgins to the lake and squinted.

Someone was on the ice.

He did a double take.

A figure skater, wearing black—except for her skates and a multicolor beanie—glided across the ice. Her graceful movements with outstretched arms and fast spins reminded him of the ice show his grandmother dragged him to when he was twelve. He'd gotten snacks, which made the two hours pass quicker, but he would have rather watched the Mariners or Seahawks. That was well before the Volcanoes, an expansion hockey team, arrived in Seattle.

No music played, yet she skated as if performing for a packed arena. She…captivated Elias.

The skater must have tucked her hair inside the beanie, and he wanted to know what color her hair was. Eyes, too, but he stood too far away.

And then he remembered…

Higgins!

The dog sat facing the skater.

Elias took a slow, careful step and then another. The dog didn't flinch.

Only another two feet to go. Snow crunched under his left foot. He inhaled sharply.

Higgins bolted across the ice directly in the path of…

"Stop!" Elias yelled.

Neither the dog nor skater listened. The leash slid across the ice right in front of the skater, who skated with her chin up.

"Be careful!" Elias shouted.

The scene played out in slow motion. Higgins froze. Her right skate hit the leash, and she stumbled. The skater tried to keep her balance by sticking her arms out, but her action didn't stop gravity. She hit the ice with a thud.

Higgins jumped on top of her and licked her face.

The skater laughed. She reached into her jacket pocket. "Well, this is a first. Where did you come from, cutie?"

Her voice wrapped around Elias, as warm and comfortable as a fleece blanket. He wanted to hear it again, only he wanted her to speak to *him*.

He stepped onto the ice, taking small steps to keep from falling. "Are you okay?"

The skater looked at him.

Gorgeous green eyes. Elias's mouth went dry. He nearly fell flat on his back.

Forget speaking. All he could do was breathe.

"Is this your dog?" she asked.

"Sorta." He came closer, unsure why he found himself so tongue-tied. A friend from law school had once told Elias that dogs were a chick magnet. But Higgins running into this woman seemed more like luck. "I'm fostering him for the holidays."

She rubbed Higgins with a gloved hand. "Friendly."

"He'd been in my house for less than five minutes when he took off. I'm sorry. Did you hurt yourself?"

She grabbed onto the leash, placed Higgins on the ice, and carefully stood. "I've taken much harder falls over the years, but thanks for the concern."

"You skate a lot?" he blurted.

"Yes." The amusement in her voice matched the

twinkle in her eyes. "Not a fan of the sport?"

He shrugged. "I prefer hockey."

"Of course, you do." She appeared more resigned than upset. "Here you go."

He took the leash from her. "Thanks. I'm Elias."

She hesitated. "Tasha."

Tasha. The name suited her. "You're not from around here."

Tasha brushed off the snow from her backside. "No."

Only locals came to this part of the lake unless… He remembered seeing a car he didn't recognize drive by when he'd brought in the mail before he ate lunch. "You're staying in the last cottage on Pinewood Lane."

Tasha stiffened, and her eyes narrowed. "How do you know that?"

"I live in the second house on the right. The one you're in is the only rental on the lane."

That might change. Dalton Dwyer had bought the cottage where Tasha was staying and would take possession in January. No one knew Dalton's plans for it yet. Some thought he would relocate from Portland since he'd grown up in Berry Lake, but the guy was in real estate and business development so the property might just be an investment.

She laughed. "Small towns are always the same."

"Everyone knows your business."

Tasha nodded. "Aren't you freezing out here?"

Elias wasn't wearing a jacket, but somehow, he was warm. "I ran after Higgins, so I'm not cold."

"Higgins." Tasha's face brightened, taking his breath away. "What a cute name. Is he named after Henry from *Pygmalion* or the one from *Magnum P.I.* or the guy in *Ted Lasso*?"

Who knew Higgins was such a popular name? Elias scratched his chin. "I don't know. The rescue told me that was his name from his…person, who died."

Tasha bent over and petted Higgins. "I'm so sorry, sweetie."

The dog soaked up the attention.

Elias didn't blame him, but they shouldn't stand around in the cold for too long. "I should get him home."

"I was about to head inside too." She glanced at the dog, but she kept smiling. "Before…"

He laughed. "Higgins and his leash got in the way."

"I can skate more later." She moved her skates back and forth. Either she was cold or bored. "The loving having ice right next door. If only there were lights…"

"If you want to skate at night, there's a temporary rink set up in the park. It's open until eight during the week and nine on weekends."

"You know a lot about it."

"I'm on our town's Winter Extravaganza committee. The rink is my responsibility."

"You've piqued my curiosity. I'll have to check it out."

"Please do. The proceeds benefit local nonprofits, including the Berry Lake Animal Rescue. I'm fostering Higgins as part of their Home for the Holidays program." Elias was rambling, but he wouldn't deny his curiosity about, and attraction, toward Tasha. A holiday romance might be fun. "Well, nice meeting you. If you need anything…"

"Second house on the right." She waved to Higgins. "Bye."

She didn't wait for a reply and skated off.

Elias hoped he saw her again soon. He watched to see if Tasha was injured, but she skated like a pro. Impressive, but he didn't want her to think he was a creeper, so he headed off the ice. His shoes slid, but he kept his balance.

"Be glad I didn't fall. And that you didn't hurt Tasha or yourself." Elias glanced at Higgins.

The dog didn't appear guilty. If anything, Higgins had added a bounce to his step.

"Don't play innocent with me. No more running away." Elias kept his tone firm. "You're a guest. A temporary one. Don't wear out your welcome, or you'll find yourself at the rescue faster than I can say, Marmaduke."

Four

After skating, Tasha finished unpacking. The cottage was well-furnished with comfortable, overstuffed furniture and sturdy wood tables. She glanced at the Christmas tree in the corner. The decorations were tasteful, but its presence annoyed her. She wanted nothing to remind her of the upcoming holiday. Yet a lighted garland was draped across the stone fireplace, and a single red stocking hung from the mantle. *TASHA* was embroidered on the white cuff.

"Maybe the property manager will let me take down the decorations." She would call on Monday. No need to bother them over the weekend.

As if on cue, her cell phone rang. Her brother's name lit up the screen.

With a smile, she took the call. "I thought you had a game today."

"We do. You'd better watch."

"I will." She enjoyed watching him play. Someone shouted in the background. He must be in the locker room. "You shouldn't have gone to so much trouble."

"What do you mean?"

She didn't buy his confused tone for a second and ran her finger over her name on the stocking. "The cottage is decked out for the holidays."

"You wanted a white Christmas. I have no control over the weather, but I had some sway with the property management company. You might not want the halls decks, but in a couple of weeks, you'll be glad I did what I did, so don't call to get rid of them."

The guy knew her too well, but then again, they had that twin bond. Still, she felt compelled to defend herself. "Did I saw I was doing that?"

"No, but you thought it." Alek laughed.

She wouldn't give him the satisfaction.

"You've got to admit, it's a nice touch," he added.

"You'll make someone a great husband."

He laughed. "Not until I retire."

"Can't keep away from the puck bunnies."

"Supermodels and singers," he said a beat later.

"You'll change your mind when you meet the right woman."

"After I retire," Alek repeated.

"Stop being a diva, Ransom, and set a better example for the rookies," a male voice bellowed through the cell phone. "Hit the ice now."

"Gotta go, sis. Love ya."

"Love you." Tasha disconnected from the call.

The rest of the day was hers to do whatever she wanted. A meal out sounded good.

Her cell phone buzzed with a text notification. Had Alek forgotten to tell her something? She glanced at her phone.

Mom: Let's compromise. You stay in that small town until the 23rd. Then you meet us at your brother's place on Christmas Eve.

That wasn't a compromise. That was Mom trying to get what she wanted. Tasha groaned.

Forget eating. She needed a nap.

* * *

That evening, a pot of pasta sauce simmered next to a large pot of noodles boiling in Elias's kitchen. He'd spend the day trying to get used to having a dog in the house. That meant practicing commands, which Higgins knew, playing fetch, which the dog appeared to enjoy, and figuring out what being a foster dog parent meant, which he still didn't have a clue.

He realized one thing, however. Higgins had separation anxiety whenever Elias went into the garage or to the bathroom and closed the door. The dog's whimpering about ripped his heart out of his chest. So Higgins had followed Elias everywhere as if he would suddenly vanish.

Elias might have to ask Sabine if there was anything he could. Did doggy psychiatrists exist? Maybe Roman Byrne, a local veterinarian could help. For now, Higgins sat at Elias's feet, appearing content.

"Hungry?"

A tail wag was the response.

Elias reread Sabine's instructions and placed them on the counter. He glanced at the time.

"Ten more minutes. Then you can have dinner."

Higgins panted.

The panting wasn't new, but Elias didn't know if it was normal. He checked the instructions to find nothing about panting. Maybe the dog was dehydrated.

He pointed at the full water bowl. "Drink some water if you're thirsty."

The dog didn't move.

"Well, you know where the water is if you want a drink."

The timer beeped. Elias checked the pasta and poured the contents of the pot into a colander. He'd made more than he needed. "I could have invited someone over and still had enough leftovers for lunch."

Though not just someone.

Tasha.

He appreciated how polite she'd been after Higgins's leash tripped her. She was also beautiful, and her smile…

Elias shook the thought from his head. He had a foster dog and the ice rink to supervise. The Christmas show fundraiser for the community fund, which supported local nonprofits, was also on his task list, but he kept hoping someone else would step up.

Higgins barked and ran toward the front door.

Interesting. The dog mustn't be hungry.

A knock sounded.

Or there was someone at the door.

Elias made his way over to the entryway, scooped the dog into his arms, and opened the front door. He did a double take. "Dad?"

Dad didn't wait for an invitation. He held onto a bag and pushed past Elias into the house.

A sarcastic remark wanted to come out, but Dad was in the living room already. Elias closed the door and set Higgins on the ground.

Surprisingly, the dog remained next to him.

"I went into the office today." Dad pulled out a stack of folders. "These were on my desk."

Elias crossed his arms over his chest. "They're the cases you gave me. The same ones you knocked off my desk. I don't have time to do them."

"Tonight?"

Saying it was the weekend would do nothing.

Instead, he shook his head. "I have to be at the ice rink when it closes tonight. And I'm supervising the volunteers tomorrow."

Dad muttered something under his breath. "You're probably happy you have to neglect your job."

Most people in town thought Elias was so lucky to have a father like Marc Carpenter, who had taken been at his debate tournaments, hockey games, and other extracurricular activites. He'd paid for Elias's college and law school, but Elias had never asked for that. He didn't have nearly the same amount of experience as his grandfather and father. All he wanted was to be treated with respect.

Elias stood taller. "I'm not happy about it, but it's the weekend. Most people, usually you and Gramps, get Saturday and Sunday off. Why shouldn't I, even though much of it will be spent at the rink?"

Or with Higgins.

"You must pay your dues."

"I've paid them long enough here. I shouldn't be made to feel bad for taking a weekend off. And that's one question I'll be asking when search for a new position."

Dad's face paled, the same way it had the other night, but he recovered quickly. "Words are easy to say. Your grandmother—"

"Wants me to be happy." Dad had a good poker face. That was crucial when standing in front of a judge, but the tick at his jaw gave him away. "She wants me to meet a nice woman and settle down. Don't you remember her trying to get me to take out one of Sabine's daughters? But it's impossible to have a serious relationship when I'm doing the work of three attorneys."

Dad didn't say a word, but his nostrils flared.

Elias didn't blink.

A standoff. Sometimes he and Dad were too similar.

But Higgins needed to have dinner. So did Elias. "I made pasta for dinner. Have you eaten yet?"

"Thanks, but I'm heading over to your grandparents." Dad glanced at Higgins. "I'll see you at work on Monday."

With that, Dad left. He took the bag with the files.

That was odd. Elias half laughed. "Looks like more progress."

* * *

After skating in the morning and spending a lazy day watching two Christmas movies, Tasha decided to go to town. It was late afternoon, and she could see the town and eat dinner out. Something she hadn't done yesterday.

She put on her beanie and gloves, locked the front door, and got into her car. The town of Berry Lake was on the other side from her slice of heaven on Pinewood Lane. She couldn't wait to see the shops that Selena had told her about, but Elias's words also played on an endless loop.

If you want to skate at night, there's a temporary rink set up in the park.

She didn't know which appealed to her more—the ice rink or his rich-as-hot-chocolate-topped-with-whipped-cream voice.

What was she thinking?

It had to be the rink. Skating was in her blood. Even she no longer performed, being a figure skater defined her. She would use her time in Berry Lake to decide if it still did.

I live in the second house on the right.

As she drove toward the stop sign, Tasha didn't allow her gaze to drift. She focused on the black asphalt clear of snow ahead of her. It didn't matter where Elias lived or if he was home. She gripped the steering wheel as if her hands controlled where she looked.

"Turn right on Lakeshore Drive," the voice on her map app directed.

Tasha blew out a puff of air as if to rid thoughts of Elias from her mind and loosened her fingers. "Glad you know where I'm going because I don't have a clue."

That was usually the case. While traveling, but these days, also in life. She had no idea where she was going or how to get there. Having GPS was at least one less thing she had to sort through.

Tall evergreens with snow-laden branches stood at attention. Sunlight glistened off the snow as if a million crystals had been carried by the wind and dropped there. The way the light filtered through the trees gave the scenery a magical feeling.

A sigh welled inside of her.

As a little girl, she'd dreamed of escaping to Narnia, but who needed a wardrobe to go there? Unnecessary in Berry Lake. The road had transported her to somewhere better—somewhere real.

She spotted a brown boat-ramp sign up ahead. The metal post reminded Tasha of Elias's blue-gray eyes. The color was a unique blend, and she wouldn't mind getting a closer look. As they'd spoken, she appreciated the kaleidoscope of emotion playing in them.

Had he noticed me gawking at him earlier?

Probably not, but the way Elias had run after Higgins without putting on a jacket or hat warmed her better than the dashboard's vents. He'd put his foster dog's safety above his comfort level. That touched Tasha's heart.

She wouldn't have minded touching his wavy, light-brown hair to see if the strands were as soft as they appeared. However, his easy grin had been her favorite—and it was contagious, making her realize how long she'd been faking smiles.

Does he have a girlfriend?

She hadn't noticed a ring, but some married men didn't wear them. That didn't mean…

Stop.

Tasha turned on the radio. Static. She pressed the scan button to find another station. The only thing besides news and sports was Christmas music. Oh, well. "Sleigh Ride" was better than listening to her ridiculous thoughts. But not even the jingling bells silenced a question.

Why was she fixating on Elias?

She wasn't in Berry Lake to meet anyone. Her life was a hot mess. Before she considered a romance or even a flirtation, she needed to figure out what came next.

"Turn right," her map app directed. "Your destination is on the left."

No more thinking about him.

Tasha parked on a quiet street lined with tall trees, quaint houses decorated with lights, and inflatable Santa figures on snow-covered front yards. Okay, she wasn't into Christmas this year, but everything about Berry Lake was better than she'd imagined. And she'd imagined a lot.

"I feel like I'm in a movie, and I haven't even seen Main Street yet."

She touched the spot over her heart. The beat against her palm was solid and steady. Exactly how she wanted it to be.

Tasha slid out of the car and hit the key fob to lock the doors.

She inhaled deeply, filling her lungs with the crisp, chilly air. The sharp pine—a smell like outside the cottage—tickled her nose and reminded her of past Christmases with her family when they had a live tree, but no homesickness followed.

The temperature had dropped since she'd skated earlier. Tasha tugged her beanie lower over her ears and adjusted the scarf around her neck.

Arrow-shaped signs with poles decorated with garland and red ribbon pointed in the direction of the ice rink.

As she entered the park, Christmas carols and laughter increased in volume with each step she took. Lights hung in trees, giving the place a theme park feel. More lights lined the trailer with skate rentals and along the edges of a tent where Santa sat in a sleigh and elves took photographs of kids visiting him.

Tasha spun to take in all the sights. The atmosphere screamed holiday, and a weight pressed against her heart. Ice rinks and arenas filled towns and cities across the globe, yet she longed for hers—well, Mom and Dad's. Actually not even theirs anymore. But she hadn't come to Berry Lake to mope. The setup gave her ideas for Wishing Bay if the new owners demolished the old rink. See, going there was the right decision.

People of all ages skated. A little boy dressed in a multicolored-striped snowsuit pushed a skate trainer on the ice. An older couple holding lidded cups, their shoulders pressed against each other, sat on a bench. Two teenaged boys zigged in front of a family of four. Three girls around twelve, clinging to each other with their ankles turning in, skated with beaming faces. Enthusiasm made up for what they lacked in skills.

"Hey, Tasha," a man called.

Her pulse sped up as if attempting a quad. She knew who that was.

A practiced smile slid into place. A smile not even her family could tell was fake. More than one person had suggested Tasha become an actress. Little did they know, she'd been acting her entire life.

She turned to greet Elias, who wore the same pants as before, but he'd added a parka, gloves, hat, and boots. His eyes were gorgeous up close. Butterflies unleashed in her stomach. Nope. She needed them to return to their cocoons.

Now.

Tasha released the breath she'd been holding. "Hi."

"Checking out the rink?"

"You piqued my curiosity."

Standing taller—and dare she say prouder—Elias motioned to the ice. "What's the verdict?"

Her opinion had formed a nanosecond after

arriving, but she didn't answer. Instead, she watched him shift his weight from foot to foot like an impatient kid. It was all sorts of adorable.

Time to put him out of his misery. "It's wonderful. Magical."

His grin lit up his face brighter than all the colored lights on the rink's sideboards. "I'm happy you think so."

"The rink is a nice size. Not as big as the one in Bryant Park, but Berry Lake isn't New York City."

His eyebrows shot up. "You've skated at Bryant Park?"

She'd not only skated there but also performed. Rockefeller Center too. "It was a while ago."

Not a lie. Three years wasn't that recent.

He shoved his hands into his jacket pockets and then removed them. "I haven't skated since I was a teenager."

"What's stopping you now?" she asked.

"No idea. Especially with the money going to a good cause."

She peered around him. "The line for skates isn't long."

Elias glanced over his shoulder. "That's the shortest it's been compared to earlier."

"Nothing to stop you."

"Except I might fall flat on my face."

She couldn't tell if he was making an excuse or not.

"Everyone falls. I did this morning. No big deal."

"You fell because of Higgins. You wouldn't have otherwise."

Ninety-nine percent true—because slips happened to everyone—but she wouldn't admit that aloud. "Skate."

He opened his mouth and then closed it. "If you'll skate with me."

Yes. Desire hit hard and fast. The joy coming from the rink was palpable. But self-preservation warned against it. "I…can't."

"Come on," Elias urged in a playful tone. "I can tell you want to."

Tasha did, but his recognizing that surprised her. The only problem? She hadn't skated in public—outside of choreographing—in three years. Berry Lake might be a small town—with fewer people than Wishing Bay—but she no longer wanted to be in the limelight. Not that anyone would recognize her. She'd retired after Worlds, nearly three years ago.

She struggled with what to say. "I do, but…"

"No buts. I don't know what to do out there. It's been that long." The words rushed out. He didn't even stop for a breath, but she discerned each one. "Follow me."

This was a bad idea, not as bad as eating an entire bag of kettle corn during a Christmas-in-July movie binge, but she wanted to skate.

Skate, not skate with him.

Tasha fell in step beside him. "You're persuasive."

"I have to be." He led her toward the rental trailer. "I'm a lawyer."

Her only interactions with lawyers had been with those from the sports agency that had once represented her. "Do you work long hours?"

"Yes, but Higgins's arrival got me the weekend off." Elias rubbed his palms together. "I'm ready to play until Monday."

His flirty tone reaffirmed what a lousy idea skating with him was. Because she enjoyed seeing that side of him and having it directed at her. She gulped. "Shouldn't you be with Higgins?"

Elias stood in line behind a family of five. "He's at home adjusting to my house. I called the woman who runs the rescue to make sure it was okay to leave him since I had to check on the rink."

"You've done a fabulous job here."

"Thanks, but all I did was supervise the setup. The kudos go to the volunteers who set up and work the various shifts."

Humble. Elias appeared to be the antithesis of Drew, and her attraction was growing. Who was Tasha kidding? She wanted to be a magnet to his metal. A few laps and then she would tell him goodbye.

A few minutes later, Tasha held a pair of rental skates. She hadn't planned on skating. Coming here had been purely a scouting missing until bumping in Elias. She tied the rental skates' laces. Her feet already hated these boots. She stood. "Ready?"

Elias finished tying his skates. "No, but I've never let that stop me."

I wish I could say the same thing.

Once upon a time, with millions watching on television, she'd skated, full of confidence and courage. Nothing had frightened her. Now, hitting the ice with thirty others made her nauseous. She'd better not throw up.

"Let's go," he said.

She followed Elias. Noise and music surrounded them, but he didn't talk to her. The silence gave Tasha a chance to calm herself with deep breaths.

Her pulse slowed. If only her brain would too.

Elias stepped onto the ice. His left skate slid, but he caught himself. "Don't make me do this alone."

Tasha joined him. He struggled to gain his footing, so she held out her arm. "Hold on to me."

He did. That seemed to be the support he needed. His steps turned into glides. "I'm skating."

"You're doing great. Do you want me to let go?"

"Okay." He released her arm. Each stroke became longer, steadier. "It's like riding a bike."

"Only more fun."

Elias nodded. "I may wear skates when I supervise the rink."

A thrill shot through Tasha. She loved introducing or, in Elias's case, reintroducing ice skating. "You should."

A kid hunched low cut in front of them.

Elias stumbled.

She steadied him. "I've got you."

A skate trainer pushed into their backside, and Tasha went down. So did Elias. She landed half on the ice and half on him. He was solid, suggesting he must find time to work out.

"Are you okay?" she asked.

He laughed. "Who knew kids were more dangerous than the ice itself?"

"Dogs too." Tasha stood. "Two falls in one day for me."

"You win." He went to stand, slipped, and hit the ice. "Guess we're tied now."

"To stand, go on all fours." She ignored his are-you-kidding-me expression. "Bring one knee up, so you're kneeling."

Mischief filled his eyes. "Like I'm proposing?"

No way did she want the image of him pulling out a ring in her head. "Like taking a knee in a football or soccer game."

He kneeled. "What do I do next?"

"Put a hand on the bent knee to stabilize yourself and use the other hand to push against the ice while you stand."

He did that and stood. His lips parted. "It works."

"Yes, but we need to move, or you'll be practicing that again when someone takes us out."

"All the kids think they're speed skaters."

"That's better than pretending to be a hockey player and checking people."

"We might see a couple of those. In September, Logan Tremblay from the Seattle Volcanoes bought a lake house, so he's a popular guy in town."

Logan was a good influence on Alek, who needed to stop dating women as if they were library books, needing to be returned by a due date. "He's a fantastic hockey player and person."

Elias nodded. "He and his wife, Selena, recommended installing an ice rink."

"It's a great idea."

Another nod. "It depends on how things go, but the rink might become an annual event."

"Traditions like that are part of a small-town holiday." Even without snow, Wishing Bay still had memorable events to make the holiday special. The cookie swap was one of her favorites. The Nativity on Ice show had been her favorite, but people would quickly forget that tradition like they had forgotten the rides in the town's fire truck when she'd been younger.

In the center of the rink, a young girl prepared to spin but fell on her bottom. She slapped the ice with her gloved hands and then wiped her eyes.

Oh, no. Tasha understood the frustration well. She motioned to the skater. "Do you mind if I help her?"

"Go ahead," Elias said.

She glided over to the girl. "Want help?"

As the girl nodded, her lower lip stuck out. "My mom showed me a video on how to do a spin, but it's not working. All I do is fall. And fall. And fall again."

"Learning to fall the right way is an important skill to have." Tasha told her the easy way to get up from the ice and waited for the girl to stand. "Have you learned a two-footed spin?"

"No."

"Let's have you try that, then." Tasha showed the moves. "Stand straight. Be sure to keep your head up and hold out your arms."

The girl did everything Tasha had said. "Like this?"

"Yes, now march, so you turn in a circle, then you stop marching as you bring your arms in and…" Tasha spun. "Voila."

An awe-filled expression stared up at her. "I want to do it."

"Me too," Elias chimed in from behind Tasha. "If there's room for one more."

"There is," Tasha encouraged. "People practice tricks and spins in the center part."

After a few attempts, the girl spun. She stopped and raised her hands above her head. "I did it."

Elias tried and spun. "Me too."

"Great job." People stared at them. Maybe they wanted to learn too. "Please be careful in the rental skates. They aren't the best for spins and jumps."

The girl nodded so fast she resembled a bobblehead. Then she did another two-footed spin.

Tasha glanced at Elias. "My job is done here."

"You're a talented skater and a wonderful teacher." His gaze met hers, sending goose bumps prickling her skin. "Thanks for showing me how to get up and spin."

She stood taller, basking in the praise.

Tasha should look away, break whatever drew them together, but she didn't want to. It had been so long since she felt a potent attraction like this. She didn't want this connection to end.

Not smart.

She was finished with handsome men. Men in general. Elias wasn't Drew, but he had that same confident air. Falling for him, whether in like or in love, would be a mistake because opening her heart to anyone only led to disappointment and hurt.

Tasha swallowed. "We should—"

Someone screeched. "Oh, my goodness. That's Tasha Ramson."

The nausea returned with a vengeance. Tension formed between Tasha's shoulders.

There goes my peaceful small-town Christmas.

But she had only herself to blame.

Five

A dozen people crowded around Tasha with requests for photos and autographs. Elias recognized most, but that didn't stop his protective instinct from ramping into overdrive. No one was a physical threat, but the flash of panic in Tasha's eyes sent adrenaline shooting through his veins. He wanted to comfort her—keep her safe. Even when the panic vanished as fast as it had appeared, he wanted to do that.

She wasn't okay.

Her breath came in rapid huffs, and even though she wore a smile, it wasn't genuine. Elias leaned closer to her. "I'll get you out of here."

She replied with a slight nod. If he hadn't been paying attention, Elias would have missed it.

"Everyone not skating is in the way." He used his

in-front-of-the-judge voice. "Either start moving or get off the ice."

Gigi, a local teenager, held out her phone. "We want a selfie with Tasha."

Her best friend, Belle, nodded. "Is Alek here?"

"The Volcanoes are on a road trip this week," someone behind them said. "They're on a winning streak thanks to Ramson."

Belle leaned toward Tasha. "Is your family going to be in Berry Lake for Christmas?"

Elias wasn't getting into a discussion out on the ice. He placed his arm around Tasha, doing his best bodyguard impression to push his way through the crowd and lead her off the rink.

"How do you want to handle this?" he whispered.

"A few photos." She spoke so quietly he strained to hear her. "There aren't that many people."

For now.

News traveled wildfire-fast in Berry Lake. With one member of the Volcanoes part of this town via his wife, people following the team would know about Tasha's all-pro hockey-playing brother. Elias did, but he'd failed to make Tasha's connection to Alek.

"Shoes?" Elias asked.

"Let's get this over with first." Her resigned tone contradicted the smile frozen on her face.

He wanted to whisk her out of there, give her a hot chocolate, and kiss the worry from her eyes.

Whoa. Where had that come from?

The crowd got louder.

Elias clapped his hands, but the gloves muted the sound. He would have to use his voice to get people's attention. "If you want a photo with Tasha, line up. She won't be here for long."

Soon, only the four-foot-tall-and-under crowd remained on the ice. Everyone else stood in line.

Elias stayed a short distance from Tasha, his senses on alert, ready to step in if necessary. She, however, handled everything—and everyone—with grace. This clearly wasn't her first rodeo, and she impressed him with her willingness to do an impromptu meet-and-greet.

The minutes ticked by. Tasha called for the next person and greeted them as if they were her new best friend. She posed for as many photos as each wanted to take.

His respect for her soared.

But would her being famous change things? They'd only just met, but Elias had fun skating with her. He'd planned on asking her if she wanted to grab a coffee after they'd finished, but he didn't know if she would want to hang out after talking to so many people. If she didn't, he hoped skating still counted as a first date because he had ideas for other dates after that.

Uh-oh. The noise level increased. More people had shown up and stood in line. She would be here all night.

No way. He wouldn't let that happen.

The corners of her lips continued to tip upward, never wavering, but she'd been shifting her weight, lifting the left skate off the ground. Her feet must hurt.

Sam Cooper, in his deputy's uniform and hat, strolled up. He'd returned to Berry Lake in October after living and working in Seattle for a few years. "Need a hand?"

"Someone called this in?" Elias asked.

"Several." Sam half laughed. "The sheriff is on his way. He wants a photo with the ice skater."

Nothing regarding Sheriff Royal Dooley should be a surprise. The man had nearly destroyed two families with his rush to arrest a suspect after an arsonist set fire to the cupcake shop. "Slow crime day?"

"A no-crime day other than giving out speeding tickets." Sam surveyed the line. "But now we have some action. No one wants to miss out on a chance to meet Alek Ramson's twin sister."

Typical Berry Lake. "From what I hear, she's well known in her own right."

Sam glanced at Tasha, who posed with twelve-year-old Katie Byrne. "Not a figure skating fan, but she's pretty."

"Beautiful. Inside and out."

"Got it."

He glanced at Sam. "Got what?"

"You're calling dibs."

Was Elias? The answer struck fast. *Mine!* "I am."

"You deserve it for all the people you've helped." Gratitude shone in Sam's eyes, and Elias knew who that was for in the deputy's life. "Good luck."

Elias hoped he didn't need any luck.

The line had nearly doubled in length, and Tasha favored her left foot more. "I need to get her out of here before the entire town shows up."

Sam smirked. "Use the white steed that matches your shining armor."

"Ha-ha." Elias picked up her shoes. "Ready to play the heavy?"

Sam tipped his deputy's hat. "Always, but you're buying the next round at Sasquatch's."

The bar sat on the opposite end of Main Street from the park. Most people called it Bigfoot's to the chagrin of the owner. But locals went there to watch sports with friends, drink beer, and eat greasy food. "You're on."

"I haven't used my crowd-control skill here. A good thing I had plenty of chances in Seattle."

A bullet had grazed Sam, and other "stuff" had gone down that few outside the police department knew about. He'd reached out for advice from Elias.

"Glad you moved home."

"Me too." Sam straightened his uniform parka. "Watch the master at work."

Elias shook his head.

Sam cleared his throat. "Can I have your attention, please? It's great to see how excited everyone is to meet Ms. Ramson, but she's been at the rink long enough."

People groaned.

Sam held up his hand. "I get it, and I'm sorry, but Elias will see if Ms. Ramson has time in her schedule to come back another day."

A few frowns turned upside down, but Tasha's expression remained the same. Elias glimpsed a hint of relief in her eyes. Something he wouldn't have noticed if he hadn't been looking so closely.

"Go skate or head home," Sam said. "Thank you."

The line dispersed, though a few people lingered.

Tasha posed for a final photograph with a man Elias didn't recognize. He must be from out of town. "Nice to meet you," she said before the guy walked away.

"Do you need anything, Ms. Ramson?" Sam asked.

"No, thanks…" She squinted at Sam's chest—where his last name was embroidered on a patch. "Deputy Cooper."

Sam nodded. "I'll stick around until you leave to make sure you aren't bothered."

"It's not a bother, but I appreciate it." She lifted her left foot.

Elias held up her boots. "Ready for these?"

"Please, but…" Tasha glanced around. "The benches are full, but I've done this standing up before."

"No need." Elias kneeled in front of her and unlaced her skates. "I've got this."

"Such service." Tasha sounded pleased.

"This way you'll tell everyone how much you enjoyed your stay in Berry Lake, so others visit." Elias was only half joking. He wanted to make himself memorable to her so she would return. Weird, but he'd never felt such an instant connection with anyone as he did with her.

"That's our Elias." Sam snorted. "He's not only the best lawyer in town, but he's also the nicest. You're in good hands."

Leave it to Sam. However, his last comment would earn the deputy a second round the next time they met up for drinks. Elias pulled off the left skate. A sock-covered foot shouldn't be so attractive. He forced himself not to touch her. Instead, he positioned her boot so she could step into it.

She did. "Thanks for the testimonial, deputy."

Sam clucked his tongue. "Though I've got to say, Elias is doing this wrong."

"Am not." That was his usual reply when Sam joked around.

"The prince is supposed to put Cinderella's glass slipper on her foot," Sam teased. "Not take it off."

"Trust me." Tasha wiggled her right skate. "I want both off A-S-A-P."

Elias did as she asked. When he finished, he stood

and brushed his hands together. "Now, we can get out of here."

"Not so fast, Elias Carpenter." Charlene Culpepper strode up. She might not have a scepter and crown, but she ruled Berry Lake and owned Events by Charlene.

Sam stepped back as if slowly retreating from a mama bear and not wanting to startle her.

Elias didn't blame him. Charlene was a lot to handle. Nothing got past the event planner. Her network of gossip informers would make the NSA jealous.

"I'm Charlene Culpepper, and you must be exhausted," she said in a comforting voice to Tasha. "You and Elias should come over to my place for a few minutes. You can rest and warm up while the crowd dies down. I've got hot tea or hot chocolate and cupcakes from our very own Berry Lake Cupcake Shop."

Tasha's glance met Elias's. "Do you have time?"

He would make time for her. "Yes."

"That sounds lovely," Tasha said. "And who would say no to a cupcake?"

Charlene beamed. "Your first day in town, and you fit in already. Let's go."

As she led them out of the park and toward Main Street where her business was located, people kept their distance. A few held up their phones.

Elias walked next to Tasha. "Sorry things got out of hand."

"It's not your fault."

He disagreed but understood why she said that. "Were you unsure about skating today because you didn't want to be recognized?"

"That's one reason."

Questions swirled like the whirlpools near the waterfall, but he would ask those later. If there was a later. He hoped so.

Charlene led them to her business, housed in a fairy-tale-worthy cottage with lights strung along the eaves. A wooden *Events by Charlene* sign stood in the yard. She opened the front door where a wreath hung and motioned for Tasha to go first. "Please excuse the mess. We're preparing for a wedding."

"Sheridan DeMarco's." Elias stepped inside and closed the door behind him.

Vanilla and cinnamon mixed with a floral fragrance, reminding him of Grammy's perfume. The overstuffed furniture, frilly decorations, and more throw pillows than anyone needed was like the things in Grammy's parlor where she knitted and drank tea. He called her every day, if only for a few minutes, but he needed to visit and introduce her to Higgins.

"Yes," Charlene said. "It's a small wedding with a limited guest list, but a large budget."

"Sheridan told me they were inviting family and a

few close friends." Elias hadn't been upset about not getting an invitation. If anything, he'd felt a sense of relief—one less obligation in a life full of them. "Smaller is better for her under the circumstances."

Those being Sheridan's horrible father, Sal, and stepmother, Deena.

Nodding, Charlene pointed to Tasha. "I'm sure you can find someone to keep you company that day. Or sooner."

Elias shook his head. It looked like playing matchmaker to her three daughters wasn't enough for Charlene.

"Careful," he whispered.

"I'm not doing anything." Charlene kept her voice low. "But you should ask if she has any ideas for the show. Maybe she'd help."

"Shhh." However, Charlene's suggestion had merit.

The committee had been at a standstill over the Extravaganza having a show of some sort. Penelope Jones, who owned Huckleberry Inn across the street, wanted them to put on a nativity pageant. Charlene thought a holiday talent show would be fun. Sabine supported a community concert with caroling from the audience. Elias hadn't cared so long as he didn't have to do any work.

"These are lovely." Tasha stared at a table full of ornaments. She glanced over her shoulder. "Are they wedding favors?"

"Guests will receive filled stockings as favors." Charlene went over to her. "These ornaments are decorations for the flocked trees at the reception, but guests can take one home if they like."

"Handmade?"

Charlene nodded. "Hope Ryan Cooper painted them. She's a local artist, and a few of her works are at the gallery if you enjoy art."

"I do." Tasha raised her hand as if to touch an ornament and then lowered it. "Cooper? Is the artist related to the sheriff's deputy?"

"His sister-in-law," Charlene answered before Elias could. "Take a seat, and I'm going to run to the kitchen to grab the refreshments."

Tasha sat on the love seat. "I'm from a small town, and I just realized they really are all the same."

Elias took the spot next to her. "Everyone is related, dated, or is in a longtime feud."

"Yes, but I like that, though it can feel suffocating after a while."

"Nothing wrong with making a change."

She nodded. "You can always go back."

It was his turn to nod.

She rubbed her palms against her pants. "You and Charlene were whispering."

"Guilty." Might as well ask. He angled his shoulders toward Tasha. "Charlene and I are on the Winter Extravaganza committee."

Tasha's lips parted. "That's why you're overseeing the rink."

He nodded, happy Tasha remembered. "We can't decide on one event."

"What's that?"

Elias fought the urge to scoot closer. Something about Tasha drew him in. He understood how the trout he caught in Berry Lake must have felt. "There's supposed to be a Christmas show. It's a fundraising event. But the committee keeps going back and forth on what the show should be."

"It's the first week of December. Aren't you cutting it close?"

He shrugged. "Well, this is small scale. The committee has narrowed it down to a nativity play, talent show, or concert."

She tilted her head. "Do all three?"

Elias flinched. "Say what?"

Tasha tapped her chin with her index finger. "This is your first year having the ice rink, correct?"

"Yes."

"Our rink used to put on an annual nativity play. Though some called it a pageant. There was more to it than Mary, Joseph, the shepherds, wise men, and angels. The show featured skaters from preschool-age to teenagers. Lines and songs had to be memorized, but it wasn't complicated. Money from ticket sales went to help skaters and hockey players with travel expenses."

"The Extravaganza raises money for the non-profits in town."

"You mentioned that." She paused. "You could do something at the rink. You'd need to bring in portable bleachers and sell reserved seats, but there's room at the park."

"Great idea." But... None of the other committee members could organize something like that. The rink location would make the show his responsibility. Unless...

You should ask her to help with the Christmas performance.

Charlene was a genius. Not only could they have a holiday show that accomplished all the parts everyone on the committee wanted, but he would get to spend more time with Tasha. Well, during his non-working hours. Still, a win-win.

"That sounds great. But none of us have the experience or expertise." As Elias emphasized the last word, his throat tightened.

What was the worst thing that could happen?

Nope. He didn't want to think about that. "You're on vacation, but would you be interested in helping us put on something like you did at your old rink?"

Tasha opened her mouth and then shut it.

Lead filled Elias's stomach. He rubbed his thumb over his fingertips. "It would be smaller scale, of course, since there's not much time, and we only have the temporary rink. But we've never done anything involving skating. Just some guidance on how to coordinate the show would be a big help."

She bit her lower lip.

"Don't answer right now," he added. "Think about it."

Only, please. Please, say yes.

Six

Why am I even considering this?

Sitting on the love seat next to Elias, Tasha listened to the discussion between him and Charlene about a possible ice show. Tasha struggled to stay out of the conversation. She gave an occasional and noncommittal "hmmm" in between sips of black tea and nibbles of the peppermint chocolate cupcake.

It was…hard.

She wanted to jump in with both skates, but self-preservation told her to politely say goodbye and hide in her cottage for the remainder of the month. The less she said, the better. She needed time to decide.

Not how she expected her first weekend in Berry Lake would turn out. At least the cupcake was tasty. She took another bite and then sipped her tea.

Something buzzed.

Elias pulled his cell phone from his jacket pocket

and glanced at the screen. His features relaxed. "Sam says things are back to normal at the rink."

That was Tasha's cue to leave. She finished her cupcake and wiped her mouth. "Thanks for inviting us over, Charlene. I needed a chance to regroup."

"Anytime." Charlene beamed like a proud mama. "I hope to see you around town."

Working on the ice show was implied but not spoken.

Seriously, Berry Lake was no different from her hometown. In Wishing Bay, Phoebe McAllister appeared to have the same role as Charlene, though Phoebe preferred to call herself the town's fairy godmother. The whimsical name suited the dress shop owner perfectly. More than once, she'd waved her figurative magic wand and helped Tasha. It hadn't mattered that her youngest daughter no longer wanted to be friends with Tasha.

"Me too." Tasha stood. She wasn't an introvert, but she craved alone time.

Elias rose. "I'll go with you to your car."

Her heart bumped.

Oops. Not the reaction she wanted. Tasha enjoyed spending time with Elias, even after being interrupted on the ice. She was just peopled-out.

They left Charlene's. A large Victorian house with a turret and front porch, reminding Tasha of the Wishing Bay Dress Shop only in different colors, sat across the street. She hadn't noticed it on their way there. Wreaths hung in each window and on the door. Lights outlined the eaves and roofline. Garland wrapped around the *Huckleberry Inn* signpost.

Tasha motioned to the inn. "Pretty house."

"The Huckleberry Inn has the best breakfasts in town." Elias grinned, making him appear more like a college student than a lawyer. "If you want to eat there sometime, I'd be happy to join you."

"I'd like that." The meal would be her treat to thank him. Speaking of which… "Thanks for helping me."

And getting her out of those horrendous skates. Talk about torture devices. If, and that was a big if, she ever skated there again, she would bring her own skates. To be honest, she preferred skating without a lot of people alone. Alone on the lake was the best.

They crossed the street toward the park.

"Anytime." His brows came together. "Though I hope that doesn't happen again."

Her, either. But she wanted to tease Elias. "Skating?"

"Take-a-selfie-with-Tasha time."

That made her laugh. "Most people were there because I'm Alek Ramson's twin, but I'm used to it."

"I always wanted a brother or sister, but today I'm glad I'm an only child."

"Does all the parental pressure fall on you?"

He stiffened. "Yes, but it probably wouldn't matter how many siblings I had unless they all became lawyers."

Interesting how his posture matched his tone. There must be a story there but not today. She pointed to her car. "I'm over there."

Elias reached into his pocket, pulled out a business card, and handed it to her. "My cell phone number is on this. Call or text me when you want to get breakfast."

"I will." She waited for him to mention the show.

Tasha wanted to help him. No, the fundraiser. She wasn't interested in *him*. But he could talk her into it if he used his lawyer skills.

So what if he'd been her hero earlier? She might have almost swooned when he removed her skates. But the deputy had said Elias was a nice guy. He hadn't gone out of his way for her. He must act like that with everyone.

Her breath hitched. Tasha wished he'd gone to so much trouble because she was someone special to him. *Silly*.

"Drive safely." He glanced at the sky. "The temperatures have dropped. Watch out for ice."

"I will." The space between them crackled with tension. She didn't know what had changed, but Tasha wanted distance. She hit the button on her key fob. "You too."

Exploring the town was out, but she stopped long enough to order a to go meal from a quaint Italian restaurant. With the delicious aroma of the manicotti and garlic bread filling her car's interior, the drive home flew by. The meal was amazing, but the rest of the evening dragged by slower than sitting in the kiss and cry area with the cameras filming and waiting for free skate scores to appear.

On Monday morning, Tasha drank coffee to make up for her lack of sleep.

The worst part?

She wasn't sure how to answer Elias's question. After a full night of contemplation, all she had were tight muscles, a sore neck from listening to the angel and the devil on her shoulders, and a list of the pros and cons. One con—costumes—jumped out at her. And then she remembered. That might be an easy fix.

Time to find out. She hit a number on her phone.

"Good morning, Tasha." Phoebe McAllister's voice was like a breath of fresh air, whether in the same room or four and a half hours away. "Are you enjoying Berry Lake?"

Of course, Phoebe would know where she was. Besides her magic wand, she must have a crystal ball, or Kristen had told her.

Outside the front window, snow flurries danced as if in a real-life snow globe. "I love Wishing Bay, but Berry Lake is Christmas-card perfect. I feel like I'm staying in the middle of a Hallmark movie."

"Who's the hunky hero of your movie?" Phoebe sounded like she was smiling. "A firefighter? Newspaper editor?"

Tasha pictured Elias on his knee, removing the skate from her aching foot. "Um, lawyer?"

Phoebe laughed. "Are you asking or telling me, sweetie?"

"I'm not sure."

"Then, you'll have to find out." The line went silent. "If you're not calling for love advice, it must be something else."

Love and Elias didn't belong in the same sentence. Love at first sight didn't exist. If it did, Alek would be married to Kristen with a couple of kids by now, and Tasha would still be with Drew.

Forget about insta-love. That was only a sweeter way to describe lust.

Focus.

"Someone asked me to help with a holiday ice show for Berry Lake's Winter Extravaganza. It's a fundraiser for local nonprofits."

"Sounds like a noble cause."

"Yes, but…"

"This trip was for you to figure out your future."

"Yes." Tasha's shoulders drooped. She hadn't mentioned that to anyone, but Phoebe knew her better than most. "I'd like to help, though."

Tasha wanted to help Elias. No, the fundraiser.

"But I'm not sure if I should," she added, positive not much she said was making sense.

"You want to help because that's a part of who you are. Your love language is service, which is why you're always doing things for people you care about, even if it's not in your best interest, but theirs."

Yep. And how many times had helping blown up in her face and ended up hurting her? She didn't want to remember. But... "This is different. I don't know anyone here."

"The hunky lawyer isn't a part of this?"

"Um." Tasha blew out a breath. "He is."

"I see."

She gripped the phone. "What does that mean?"

"You like him."

"I just met him." The words shot out one on top of the other. Tasha cringed. She hadn't acted like this when she was a teenager and crushing on a classmate.

"Mm-hmm. What do you need from me?"

"Are the ice show costumes easy to get to?" Tasha asked. "I'm not sure where Kristen said you were keeping them."

"Yes, I can get to them easily. The outfits from the rink are with the off-season dresses we can't return, or ones that Kristen wants us to keep."

That took care of one of Tasha's concerns. Maybe her helping with the show would work out. "Great."

"When do you need them?" Phoebe asked.

Tasha's temperature shot up. Hadn't Phoebe heard her? "N-not yet. I haven't told them yes."

"Maybe not aloud." Phoebe chuckled. "Go on."

"*If* I do this," Tasha clarified. "I can pick them—"

"You're on vacation," Phoebe interrupted. "Email me a list of costumes you need with sizes or measurements. I'll see what I can find and send them to you. Be sure you give me the address where you're staying."

Tension released from Tasha's body. Gratitude took its place. She should have known Phoebe wouldn't let her down. Phoebe never had, which took skill when Kristen wanted nothing to do with Tasha. "Thank you."

"Anything to help a good cause."

Tasha wondered if that included her.

* * *

Me: *It's Tasha. I'm happy to help you with the ice show.*

Me: *Since you already had a nativity theme in mind, that can be easily incorporated.*

Me: *Could you arrange a meeting with the committee to discuss details?*

Hunky Lawyer: *Yes! You made my day. Thank you!*

Me: *Don't thank me yet.*

Me: *You don't know what I can do.*

Hunky Lawyer: *You can do whatever you want to.*
Me: *You're good for my ego.*
Hunky Lawyer: *Meeting on Wednesday night. 6:30 pm. Town hall.*
Me: *See you then.*

As the broccoli cheddar soup simmered on the stove, Tasha reread the text exchange with Elias. She'd typed him into her contacts as *Hunky Lawyer*, and each time she saw the nickname, Tasha laughed. Still, the name suited him. And she would joke about it with Phoebe after the New Year.

Tasha removed the tea bag from her cup of Earl Grey.

Deciding to help felt good, but something else gnawed at her. She'd been in this position before, thinking she was doing the right thing only to have a situation blow up in her face.

Given her current string of bad luck, there was a huge possibility that it could happen again. But she hoped this time would be different.

Please go right.

For her sake. For Elias's sake. For Berry Lake's sake.

* * *

Tasha said yes!

Wednesday night, Elias sat on a hard plastic chair

at the town hall. Higgins lay at his feet. After spending the day in the crate while Elias worked, the dog didn't need to stay in there any longer. He listened to Tasha's vision for the Winter Extravaganza Ice Show—tryouts, on- and off-ice practice sessions, costume fittings, a dress rehearsal, and a performance date of December twenty-third. It was a little later than usual, but they'd never been so late getting started.

On Monday, when she'd texted him, he had no idea she would arrive at the meeting so prepared. Every person on the committee appeared impressed, including Penelope Jones, whose perpetual frown had disappeared for once.

Leave it to Tasha to soften the hardest of hearts.

His gooey heart was ready to melt in a puddle at his feet. Not that Tasha could tell. But she'd been on his mind since Sunday. Before and after work, he'd taken Higgins to the lake in case she was skating, but he hadn't seen her.

You're seeing her now.

She was more beautiful than he remembered. Flutters filled his stomach as if a flock of starlings decided to migrate off-season. He had it bad.

But Elias didn't mind. Knowing Tasha would be at the meeting had made his day go by faster. He didn't complain to himself once, even if he had complained to his father about how the ice show would require him to be at the rink more.

"I'll take care of signing up volunteers to help at the tryouts, practices, and rehearsals," Sabine said from her seat in the multipurpose room where the committee was meeting. "I'd rather have more than we need than too few."

"I'll be there on the weekends." Elias couldn't commit to helping during the week because of work. He might stop by the rink each night to see how things were going, but that was a far cry from chaperoning.

Sabine nodded. "I'm sure Max can help."

"My three daughters too. But we'll need more than family members." Charlene typed on a tablet. "I'll spread the word so people show up at the tryouts on Wednesday and Thursday. I can also tell potential volunteers to email or call you, Sabine."

"The more, the merrier." Tasha's enthusiasm bubbled over in her voice and eyes. She hadn't said yes out of obligation. She wanted to do that.

That pleased Elias. Who was he kidding? He felt almost giddy.

"I'll provide treats during the practices." Penelope sat ramrod straight with her white hair pulled into a tight bun. She had to be in her eighties and was more stubborn than Sabine's rescue goats. For decades, Penelope had taught etiquette classes and would make Miss Manners appear feral.

"I'll add Tasha to the committee's email loop." Sabine scribbled on her legal pad. "Thanks for coming, everyone, and have a good night."

The four women stood. Higgins remained in place with his eyes still closed and an occasional twitch of his rear paw.

Penelope hurried toward the door. Charlene and Sabine left together.

And then there were two…

Elias's palms sweated. Too bad he couldn't blame it on the forced-air heating. But the room was far from warm. He brushed his hands over his pants. "You wowed us with that presentation."

"Thanks." Tasha slung her purse strap over her shoulder. "Higgins is out."

Elias nodded. "Napping all day must be hard work."

"I may have to test that myself."

"Do it before tryouts." Elias got lost in her eyes. The interesting part? He didn't care, but he didn't want to make Tasha uncomfortable. He forced his gaze onto Higgins. "It sounds like you won't have much time after that."

"I hope it all works out."

He didn't need to be a longtime friend to see how amazing she was. "It will."

Heat rose up her neck to her cheeks. "Thanks."

Her glance at the exit told Elias she was ready to go. He didn't want to say good night. Not when he wouldn't see her until this weekend. "I came here straight from work. I ordered a pizza to pick up on my way home. Want to come over and eat?"

He didn't want to scare her off so tried to keep it light. As if this was hanging out with him and Higgins. Casual. Chill. Comfortable.

"I haven't eaten yet." She patted her stomach. "Pizza sounds good."

"Sausage, pepperoni, and mushrooms, okay?"

"Perfect."

Elias forced himself not to pump his fist. He might feel like a twelve-year-old with his first crush around Tasha, but he needed to act his age, or he'd embarrass himself.

And her too. "Meet me at my place?"

Tasha's bright eyes and the way she leaned toward him made up for her shy smile. "Second house on the right. I'll be there."

Elias couldn't wait.

Seven

Tasha parked her car in the cottage's garage to keep from having to scrape the windows if it snowed or the temperature dropped overnight. It made the most sense with Elias's house being a short walk from there. She could have driven straight to his place, but Mom had ingrained a few etiquette lessons over the years. Never show up empty-handed was one of them. Plus, doing something would take Tasha's mind off Elias, so she wasn't as frazzled when she arrived.

The man was too handsome for his own good.

Don't think about him.

She grabbed a paper plate from the cabinet and arranged store-bought cookies and a few squares of the brownies she'd baked earlier. She strategically placed a few red-, green-, and gold-foiled Hershey Kisses on the plate and covered it with plastic wrap.

Far from fancy, but Mom said it was the thought that count.

She wondered If Elias enjoyed chocolate. *Wait.* Who didn't like chocolate?

Tasha supposed a few people didn't eat it, but she'd never met one. She unwrapped the plate and added four sugar cookies to be on the safe side.

A glance at the reflection in the microwave door sent her hand to her head to smooth the mess, aka her hair. Tasha didn't know what to call this dinner, but she shouldn't show up looking like a slob. Although she didn't want to know when her hair went from looking decent to rocking Medusa locks. She doubted that happened on the drive home.

In the bathroom, she brushed her hair. Satisfied she'd tamed the tangles, she refreshed her lipstick. Her lips tingled. The shiny gloss tasted like peppermint.

Not that anyone else would be tasting it.

Still, Tasha smiled at the result two minutes of effort brought. If she wanted to impress him, she would change clothes, but she didn't want him to think she was interested in him.

She wasn't.

No dating, remember?

Still, the fluttery sensations in her stomach suggested a crush was likely. If not underway. At least crushes were safe.

Two minutes later, Tasha put on her winterwear.

She locked the cottage's front door and set off with the plate of sweets. As her exhales hung in the air, her steps crunched on the snow. She wore gloves, but if she hadn't been holding dessert, her hands would be shoved deep into her jacket pockets.

Brrr. She'd forgotten how cold winters could be. Wishing Bay had a few freezing days but nothing like Berry Lake.

Better get used to the cold with the ice show outside.

Tasha had packed appropriate clothes for skating on the lake, but breaking the skaters into shifts so they weren't outside too long might be smart. But she would have to see how the kids did with the weather the skating auditions before deciding.

Lights—some multicolored, others white—decorated the houses, cabins, and cottages on Pinewood Lane. The festive glow gave her Christmas spirit a needed boost. She wouldn't be embracing her inner Santa anytime soon, but turning her back on everything red and green and silver and gold made no sense.

Elias's house had multicolored lights hanging along his house's eaves. Those were her favorites. Not that Christmas lights made or broke a…whatever they were. His front-door wreath with holly and pinecones reminded her of the one hanging on the Wishing Bay Dress Shop's door. She had a feeling Kristen might have made it. She was creative and crafty with a design degree from a prestigious school; she should be designing the dresses her mom sold, not simply making the purchases for the shop, but no one wanted Tasha's opinion.

Each step brought her closer to Elias's porch. As she stood in front of his door, tingles threatened to erupt. She tamped them down.

You've got this.

With a slight hesitation, she rang the bell.

Higgins barked, the sharp sound a relief.

Not a date.

Dinner.

That could count as a date.

Stop thinking.

She shifted her weight from one foot to the other and back again. Okay, she was a teensy bit nervous.

The door opened. Elias held Higgins, who squirmed in his arms, trying to get down. "Hey. Great timing. I just got home with the pizza."

"Hi." As she stepped inside, the heat wrapped around her like a blanket. A few more minutes of this, and she'd be sweating. She removed her coat and hung it on a nearby rack. Elias wore socks, so she removed her boots and left them by the door.

The sharp scent of pine hit her. A glance to her left showed a live Christmas tree with multicolored lights and bulbs sitting in the corner near the front window. A few wrapped gifts nestled beneath the branches on top of a red tree skirt with gold trim.

He shut the door and placed Higgins on the floor.

Higgins sniffed her feet, turned, trotted to the fireplace, and lay on the floor.

She laughed. The dog had made himself right at home. "Higgins knows where it's warm."

"He claimed that spot the first day. Not that I want it." Elias's long-sleeved, gray Henley made his eyes silvery blue. "You didn't have to bring anything."

Tasha handed him the plate. "If my mom found out I showed up empty-handed, I'd get a lecture."

"My grandmother taught me the same thing."

The beamed ceilings and wood floors gave the open floor plan a cozy, welcoming atmosphere. A breakfast bar with three stools separated the kitchen from the living room, making it perfect for raising a family or entertaining. The dining room in the far corner, diagonal from where she stood, could be reached through either room. The décor was done in earth tones, matching the wood and lake setting. Burning logs crackled in the river-rock fireplace. Two stockings hung from the wood mantel. One was embroidered with the name Elias. The second had Higgins spelled out in glitter glue.

None of this was what she expected from a single guy's house, but she liked it. "Lovely home."

"Thanks." Elias stood with his shoulders back and a gleam in his eyes. He was at ease, but she imagined he would make a formidable opponent in the courtroom. "I got lucky. It was a foreclosure. A former rental property that hadn't been maintained. I've been slowly fixing it up. The living space and guest bathroom are the only things finished, but I'll eventually get to the rest. Ready to eat?"

She touched her stomach. Lunch had only been a quick bowl of soup. "Yes."

"Come on."

Two plates, glasses, and silverware were set on the table along with packets of crushed red peppers, Parmesan cheese, and the pizza box.

He placed the dessert plate on the far end and pulled out a chair for her.

Handsome and with manners. An attractive combination.

If Tasha wanted a boyfriend, she could do far worse than Elias Carpenter. "Thanks."

"I have beer, milk, water, and ginger ale to drink."

"Water's fine."

Elias filled the glasses with water from the refrigerator, placed them on the table, and sat. He flipped open the pizza box's lid.

The scents of basil, oregano, and other yummy goodness drifted out. Her stomach grumbled. "Excuse me."

"Mine's about to do the same." He motioned to the box. "Help yourself."

She took two slices. "Looks delicious."

"Try it."

Tasha did. "Yum. Berry Lake has better pizza than Wishing Bay."

He took three slices. "I didn't realize it was a competition."

She startled. "It's not. Sorry, my family…"

Elias leaned toward her. "What about your family?"

"Everything's a competition. From what we do to where we eat. It's been that way my entire life."

"You're all athletes, who've won medals at world-class competitions and turned pro, so that makes sense. A person has to be driven to succeed at that level." He ate a bite.

She sat back, looking at him, not sure how to feel. "You did an internet search on me?"

His cheeks reddened, making him look younger and adorable. "I follow hockey. Everyone who does knows about your brother and your parents. I forgot about you."

She laughed. "You're not the only one."

"I didn't mean to offend you."

Was she offended? Tasha smiled. "You didn't."

He relaxed, and his lips slid into an easy smile.

Would his kiss taste as delicious as the pizza?

Oops. Not the question Tasha should be asking.

What had they been discussing? She sipped her water. Oh, right… "Now that I'm retired, when I slip into a competitive mode."

Competitions were behind her. She didn't want them to be part of her life, either. She preferred helping people, on the rink and off it.

He raised a slice. "You can't help wanting to be the best. Some people are wired that way."

She nodded, taking another bite of hers. "Are you?"

"Yes, which is why I believe it's ingrained in a person? Take staying in shape. I work out on the weekends, not even close to being a professional at anything athletic, but no matter what I d, I want to be the best."

"I see your point. But you're a lawyer. Don't you have to think that way to win cases?"

Elias wiped his mouth. "Arrogance can be a trait of those who practice law. It's one of mine, but I try to keep that at the office. I'm not sure how well I succeed at that."

Tasha appreciated his honesty. "I haven't noticed it. I'd say you're more confident than anything. And I wouldn't want a mousy attorney representing me. Give me brash, in-your-face representation."

"You have my card if you ever need my services," he joked.

"I'll keep it handy."

Laughter lit his eyes. "Happy to be your one call."

Wait. Is he flirting?

Gah. Tasha had no clue. She ate to keep from speaking.

He picked up his glass. "What brought you to Berry Lake in December?"

"I wanted a white Christmas."

"You came to the right place. So, you're on vacation for the holidays?"

A quick internet search would tell him what he wanted to know. Might as well tell him the truth since he'd been open with her.

"Yes, but I'm also unemployed." The word left a bitter taste in her mouth. She took a gulp of water. "I worked at my parents' ice rink in Wishing Bay until a few days ago. They sold it but didn't tell me until they told everyone else who worked there. It was quite a shock."

"I can't imagine. That must hurt."

Present tense. Not past. "Yes, and my brother came through in a big way. He rented the cottage for me."

Elias's gaze softened. "Is your family joining you here for Christmas?"

"No. Alek has four days off from games. He didn't want to leave town, so my parents are spending the holidays with him. Honestly, I didn't want to be around my parents this Christmas. But Seattle is the last place I want to be this December." As she realized what she'd said, heat flooded her face.

"Sorry for asking so many questions. Occupational hazard." He sounded sincere. "And I want to get to know you better."

"Same with you. But I bet you have special lawyer superpowers to pry out information."

"Guilty as charged," he admitted in a playful tone. "But I have to ask. What's so horrible about Seattle?"

Tasha ate more pizza. She'd opened the door to that question. "Long story, but I'll try to be brief. Ever hear of the Nutcracker Holiday Ice show?"

"My grandmother mentioned it. Lots of big-name skaters. It's being televised as a holiday special, right?"

Tasha nodded. "I was hired to choreograph the show. Seattle is the opening city."

"Wow."

Her face burned hotter, but she had nothing to be ashamed about. Still, the thickness in her throat made her take another sip of water. "That's what I thought at first, but two weeks later, I was let go. A more polite term than fired."

His expression hardened. The quick change in his demeanor surprised Tasha, but she assumed a determined set of his jaw and lines between his eyebrows might be his lawyer face. Still attractive, but more serious.

He leaned forward. "Washington is an at-will state, so employers don't have to give you a reason, but did they tell you why you were let go?"

"No, but another skater let it be known they didn't want to work with me and complained to the producer. I hadn't choreographed that routine on purpose because of our past, but they are a big name now and I'm…not."

"You had two big hits right after another."

"It sucked big-time." Another way of saying being fired from the ice show and the rink devastated her. "But if I were touring with that ice show, I wouldn't be in Berry Lake to help with yours."

His eyebrows drew together. "It won't be the same caliber of performers."

She shrugged. "Doesn't matter to me whether brand-new or competitive skaters audition. I'll make the best program I can."

"You will."

Tasha wished she had his confidence. Hers had been wavering since she'd been fired. "Thanks."

"You're what Berry Lake needs."

What about you?

Strike that. A new friend made the most sense. Given her circumstances, a friend might be pushing it. Still, hearing his words brought tingles. "You know all the right things to say."

"I try."

"You're succeeding." She ate more pizza to keep from making goo-goo eyes at him. "Now that I've shared a deep dark secret, it's your turn."

He finished a slice and wiped his mouth on a paper napkin. "A deep dark one, huh?"

"Any secret will do. I'm not picky."

Elias took a sip of water. "I'm considering quitting my job."

Okay, that was unexpected. "You don't like being a lawyer?"

"I love being a lawyer. It's just…" He stared off into the distance. "Working for my grandfather and dad isn't what I thought it would be. I feel like their intern. Nothing's changed since I did that for them during law school, except I passed the bar, so now I get the cases they don't want, and my workload is three times theirs."

That had to be awful. "Have you spoken to them?"

He nodded. "It's like talking to myself. I told my dad we needed more staff. So far, not one job listing has been posted. They think I can handle it all. I'm mentioning it more now. We'll see what happens."

"Can you handle it all?"

"I have been, and I thought I was just paying my dues. Except it never stopped. And now, but whether I can do all the work is beside the point. I shouldn't have to, and I don't want to do it any longer."

"I'm sorry." Tasha reached across the table but drew her hand back. They didn't know each other that well. She should comfort him with words not a touch. "Family expectations can be rough."

"You know that one too?"

Boy, do I. "My parents wanted Alek and me to follow in their footsteps. My brother with hockey and me with figure skating. The goal was for us to win gold medals."

"You won a bronze, right?"

She nodded. "Not gold, though. Which wasn't bad since I'd been a pairs skater for most of my competitive career, and that was skating individually."

"Something's wrong when you place at the winter games and it's not enough."

"It is what it is. I did win Worlds after, but it's not the same."

Elias nodded. "I feel the weight of every generation of Carpenters who went into law. Some days it can be smothering."

"It can be. I wish we didn't face that kind of pressure from our families."

He half laughed. "Same. My family loves me, though I feel more like the firm's doormat right now."

"Not a good feeling."

"The worst."

Tasha finished her pizza. "I wish I had words of wisdom, but I'm at a crossroad myself."

"Want more?"

"That hit the spot but no, thanks."

Elias closed the lid, pushed the box away, slid the plate of dessert in front of them, and removed the plastic wrap. "This looks good. What's your crossroad?"

She grabbed a brownie. "My family moved to

Wishing Bay when I was eight. I've lived in Wishing Bay for twenty years, though I traveled with skating, but now that the rink is sold… It might be time for a change. I hope when I leave Berry Lake, I'll know the answer. Do you have a timeframe to make a decision on your job?"

He also took a brownie. "I've given myself until January. If they don't hire more staff, I won't stay. I…can't."

Her issues seemed minor compared to the decision he faced. She set the brownie on her plate. "I hope it works out the way you want."

"Me, too. Thinking about quitting and leaving my hometown is weird. I've lived in Berry Lake my entire life except for when I attended college and law school. I planned to stay here forever, but I need things to change before it affects my health. I want more in my life than a job I can't stand that takes all my time."

"You deserve more."

He straightened. "I've always put my family first, but I realize I do."

Maybe some of Elias's lawyer arrogance showed outside of the office, but she didn't mind. She respected him. Years of gaslighting from Drew Maddox both on and off the ice had affected her self-esteem and well…everything. Sometimes, she wondered if not getting closure, not speaking up, had held her back. Mom and Dad had told Tasha she shouldn't go public with her side of the story. They'd been concerned about her and how the news might effect Alek's hockey career, that was just taking off back then. Her bad press had looked bad enough, but a full-out war in the public eye would've been worse. As Drew's innuendos aka lies continued over the years, she kept quiet, but now that he got her fired…

Staying quiet might not be the best thing. Alek was a superstar. Not even a spoiled skater like Drew Maddox could touch her brother now. But she didn't want to think about him with Elias right there.

Tasha reached for her glass. "I know something you should do."

"What's that?"

"Go to Wishing Bay and make a wish for what you want."

He laughed. "Is that a thing where you come from?"

"Yes." It was one of her favorite things about her town. "A legend claims if you find a piece of sea glass, make a wish, and toss the sea glass into the bay, your wish will come true."

"I'd rather keep the sea glass."

"But the wishes come true, and sea glass only sits there."

"Have you tried it?"

Tasha didn't hesitate. "It's worked for me and others."

"What did you wish for?"

"Since it came true, I can tell you. I wished to win a medal at the Winter Games." Tasha stared at the uneaten brownie before meeting his gaze. She forced a laugh, hoping it didn't sound fake. "I should have been more specific and said a gold medal. Lesson learned."

"I'll keep that in mind." He glanced at something in the kitchen. "It's not late. Want to watch a movie? You can help me eat the delicious desserts you brought."

Tasha hesitated. She'd never felt such a strong connection to someone the way she did with Elias. They had more in common than she imagined they would, and their conversation over pizza hadn't been superficial. The last time she'd felt this way with anyone had been with Drew, and that spooked her.

Tonight felt like a date.

She wanted it to be a date. That was a huge problem.

Tasha stood. "Thank you, but I need to go."

With that, she left the table and went to put on her boots and jacket.

"Tasha?" Elias called out.

She was afraid if she looked back at him, she would stay, and she…couldn't. Not now when her life was not only at a crossroads but a mess. "Good night."

And then she bolted.

Eight

"You're in a rotten mood. Difficult client?"

Elias glanced up from his monitor to see Dad standing in the doorway. "I'm busy."

The truth, but he *was* also in a foul mood. His mood had nothing to do with the ever-increasing pile of work and everything to do with one person.

Not a client.

Tasha.

Last night, he'd wanted her to stay longer. He hadn't cared if they watched a movie or each other, but then she'd bolted out of his house before even Higgins realized what was happening. That included putting on her boots and coat, which took some skill. He had no idea why she'd taken off so quickly. That left him confused.

She hadn't texted him.

Not that he'd texted her, but…

If Tasha thought she could get away that easily, she was mistaken.

Whoa.

That sounded creepy stalkerish. Which wasn't what he meant.

They clicked.

Elias didn't want to let let that go.

Something had spooked her last night. He didn't know what, but he intended to find out. That wouldn't take a drive to Wishing Bay to find a piece of sea glass to make a wish upon and toss it into the sea. He would get what he wanted by being proactive. Something he hadn't been with his family until recently.

He didn't want to make the same mistake with her.

Elias knew what he wanted with Tasha. A brief romance with Tasha would be better than none at all. Might as well go for it because he had nothing to lose.

"You're distracted."

Dad's voice jolted Elias from his thoughts. His eyes met his father's displeased gaze. "If I am, it's because of my workload, supervising the ice rink, and making sure my foster dog is thriving."

"You're paying your dues." Dad must enjoy saying that phrase, or he'd stop repeating it. "Did you read the documents from the Monroe divorce?"

"Check your inbox."

Why the firm agreed to represent a slimeball like Ezra Monroe was beyond Elias. It most likely had to do with Penelope, a longtime client who'd taken Ezra's side over her own granddaughter, Juliet. Elias, however, was team juliet all the way.

"How's the dog?" Dad asked.

"Higgins is fine. But he hates being left alone."

More so when it came to bedtime.

That meant Elias hadn't slept much since Saturday, and the lack of sleep was turning him into a zombie. He didn't know if animals suffered PTSD, but Higgins had issues. He must fear someone not coming home for him again. Knowing that hurt Elias's heart. He might not want a dog, but Higgins was a good boy. He deserved better.

Dad's jaw jutted forward. "You can't bring an animal here."

"If I need to, I will. This was your idea."

"Hire a dog walker or sitter."

"I'll look into it."

"During your lunch. You have too much to do to take time off."

"I have to run home at lunchtime to take care of the dog you asked me to foster, so my needing time off each day is your fault."

"Don't get smart with me."

Elias was good at the tit-for-tat. "No job postings have gone up."

"I haven't discussed it with your grandfather."

Of course not. Dad's unenthused tone suggested he

didn't plan to, either. Time to fire a warning shot. "You should."

Dad scoffed. "What are you going to do if I don't? Quit?"

Elias's gaze met his. "If I quit, I'll give two weeks' notice, but I have enough vacation time built up to cover that and an additional three weeks, so I physically won't have to be here for those days."

Dad's face fell. A direct hit leaving shock and fear. A moment later, his features tightened, and his nostrils flared. "Don't play games with me."

"I'm not." But if Dad thought this was a game of chicken, he would lose. "Anything else you need?"

Dad turned on his heel and stomped away, heavy footsteps echoing through the hallway.

Elias should care more than he did. All he wanted to do was be the best attorney he could be, as he'd told Tasha, but not under these circumstances.

Still, he had a job, unlike her. He couldn't imagine losing two jobs. Dad and Gramps wouldn't fire Elias unless he messed up big-time, but he hated the control he'd given up in exchange for that stability.

Not worth it.

He let those three words sink in.

Elias only hoped he didn't grow too impatient waiting for January to arrive. But he didn't have to wait that long for Tasha. He knew where she'd be on Wednesday and Thursday nights, and he would be there for at least one of them.

* * *

Wednesday night, Tasha sat between Jenny O'Rourke and Juliet soon-to-be-Jones-not-Monroe, which is how Juliet introduced herself, watching auditions at the rink. Both women, in their thirties, had volunteered, and Tasha couldn't have asked for nicer helpers. Jenny brought cupcakes from the Berry Lake Cupcake Shop, and Juliet, who worked for Charlene, had tea bags and cocoa packets and two thermoses full of hot water.

The warm drinks came in handy with the cold temperature. Charlene had dropped off an outdoor heater, but it was still chilly.

"We have one more audition tonight." Jenny sipped from an insulated paper cup. "Tomorrow's list of kids looks as long."

Juliet pulled her wool cap lower over her ears. "It'll go fast."

Wait a minute. Tasha glanced at both women. "You'll be here tomorrow?"

"Of course." Juliet's voice reminded her of a cartoon princess. She looked like royalty with her beautiful face. "Once upon a time, I dreamed of making it big in Hollywood. There's not much of that in a small town. I'm having fun tonight."

"So much fun," Jenny agreed. "My husband took our daughter to Portland for a father-daughter trip. They'll Christmas shop in between visits to the zoo and the Children's Museum. This gets me out of a quiet house. I have our cat and a foster cat to keep me company, but neither say much unless they want food or a treat."

Juliet laughed. "Same for my dog, Lucy. Though I don't have that problem at work. Charlene has never met silence."

Tasha could see that. "Well, I appreciate the help."

A skater came out onto the ice and stopped. She took a deep breath. Her exhale hung in the air. "I'm Katie Byrne. I'm twelve and an intermediate skater. I also sing."

"Excellent." Tasha glanced at Katie's form. "Skate first. If you know any spins or jumps, show us, but if not, no worries. Everyone who tries out gets a part."

Katie's expression relaxed. "Want me to go now?"

"Please."

With a smile, Katie was off. She glided with long smooth strokes into a waltz jump. Next came a one-foot spin. She circled the ice again and did a Salchow and finished up with a scratch spin.

Tasha made notes on Katie's page. "That's wonderful, Katie. Now, please sing for us."

Katie sang the song "I'll Have a Blue Christmas Without You."

Juliet sucked in a breath. Her pen dropped.

Katie's voice was clear and not pitchy.

For a small town, the level of talent surprised

Tasha. Several did basic jumps and spins. One teenager, a young woman named Belle, who'd been at the rink on Saturday afternoon, had mastered double jumps and would make the perfect angel for the final nativity number.

Katie finished the song and bowed.

The three judges, as the kids had called them, clapped. Tasha wanted each child or teen to leave thinking it'd been a positive experience.

"Thank you for auditioning," Tasha said. "I'll post the cast by Friday night on the town's website."

"Thank you." As Katie skated off the ice, she practically bounced.

Juliet wiped tears from her eyes. "Oh my."

Tasha touched Juliet's arm. "Are you okay?"

Juliet nodded. She blew out a breath. "That song Katie sang packed a punch. Her parents were killed earlier this year. She and her uncle moved to Berry Lake in September. I live next door to them. I had no idea she knew how to skate or sing like that. She never said anything, and Roman never mentioned it."

"She may need time, or he might not know, or both," Jenny chimed in. "You were young when your parents died. I was in my twenties, but your world shifts when you lose them, no matter what age you are. The fact Katie auditioned is a promising sign she's adjusting to her new life in Berry Lake."

Tasha nodded. She wrote *Mary* on Katie's form. "Yes, it is."

"That's it for the Wednesday tryouts, ladies." Sabine had been herding the kids auditioning. "We can call it a night."

"Until tomorrow," Jenny joked.

Tasha glanced around, hoping to see Elias. She thought he would come by to check the rink after he got off work, but she hadn't seen him. Maybe tomorrow.

She would text him a *thank you for dinner*. That was the modern-day equivalent of a thank-you card, right?

"But seriously," Jenny continued. "Thank you for doing this, Tasha. I can't ice-skate, but I love watching it. After seeing the kids' tryouts, I can't wait to see the show."

"Same." Juliet's smile returned. "It'll be amazing."

On Thursday afternoon, the atmosphere crackled with anticipation.

Tasha loved seeing so many smiling faces. Kids auditioned one after another. The process went smoother that day without needing as much time between the tryouts. Sabine had the routine down.

The ice-skating levels varied from putting skates on for the second time to spins, but the level of singing, ranging from can't carry a tune to giving her chills, told her to add more songs to take advantage of the vocal talent. The show would encapsulate the spirit of the season—the joy the holiday brings, awakening on Christmas morning full of excitement.

A teenager named Bentley finished singing "Last Christmas" and bowed. The guy had little skating talent, but his singing made up for it. She got chills.

Tasha and the other two clapped. "And it's a wrap."

"I'm even more excited about the show." Jenny's face glowed under the lights surrounding the rink. "I wish Briley was old enough to take part."

Juliet grinned. "If this is as popular as I think it'll be, the holiday ice show will become an annual event, and Briley can try out when she's older."

Was Juliet correct? Were they creating a town tradition?

But who would run it next year? Tasha realized that wasn't her problem. She needed to get through this show and figure out her future before she worried about a town she might never visit again after she left.

Jenny laughed. "Look who shows up now that the hard work is done."

"What can I say?" Elias approached the table with Higgins on a leash. "We didn't want to miss out on all the fun."

Tasha's heart bumped. In an overcoat, pants, and expensive shoes, he was dressed for work. Well, except for Higgins being with Elias. He'd never replied to her text.

Okay, it had only been a day. Twenty-four hours.

And he was there. That had to be a good sign, right?

Not that she was looking for signs.

He flashed a charming grin that sent her heart galloping like a horse pulling a sleigh. "I have impeccable timing."

Higgins barked as if to answer too.

"My dog agrees." Elias bent over to give the dog a pat.

"Your dog?" Juliet's eyebrows shot up. "Don't you mean foster dog?"

"To-may-toes, to-mah-toes," Elias joked.

"Good boy." Jenny scratched behind Higgins's ears. "Yeti doesn't know what to make of our foster cat, Nova. She's the sweetest, diluted tortie. Briley loves her already. Dare and I do too. I'm not sure we'll return her to the rescue on the twenty-sixth."

"Do you have to?" Tasha asked.

"No, we're allowed to adopt her." Jenny patted the dog. "Which is probably the entire point of Sabine's Home for the Holidays program."

"I hope it works out for you, but I won't be a foster failure." Elias brimmed with confidence. "Higgins is a great dog, but he doesn't like being left at home while I work. I spend my lunch hour there, but he might be happier with someone who is around more."

"Or he might not." Juliet said what Tasha had been thinking. "Dogs adapt quickly. Mrs. Vernon was home most of the time, but Lucy's fine with me being gone for work and parties. Give Higgins time."

"I will, but he's not staying with me." Elias glanced around. "How did tryouts go?"

Tasha grinned at his change of subject. It felt good to have a genuine smile on her face. "Berry Lake contains a treasure trove of talent."

Juliet stood. "I'll see you at the first practice."

"I'll try to make as many as I can." Jenny rose. "Dare and Briley are home from their trip, so I'm taking off."

"Go. Both of you." Elias shooed them away. "I'll help Tasha clean up."

As Juliet and Jenny left, Tasha folded the three chairs and carried them to the skate-rental trailer. Elias followed with the table.

"Thanks." Tasha didn't like how breathless she sounded. "I hope your week is going well."

"It is. Busy as usual, but now I have a dog." He didn't sound like he was complaining. More like explaining. "Sorry I didn't reply to your text or get in touch earlier."

"No problem." It wasn't.

Or rather, it shouldn't be.

She enjoyed meeting people and making herself useful. Doing that lit her up inside. So what if being with Elias had the same effect?

"Higgins has been having problems with his crate. He won't sleep in it at bedtime. He barks and whines, and I've slept little until last night."

"That has to be rough." Tasha didn't function well without at least seven hours of sleep. "But what changed yesterday?"

A guilty expression crossed Elias's face. "I didn't make him go into the crate."

"Where did he sleep?"

"On my bed."

That seemed a big turnaround from his he's-going-back-to-the-rescue stance. "Whatever works."

He nodded. "I was desperate."

What Deputy Cooper had said about Elias was the one hundred percent truth. He was a nice guy.

"Higgins and I are about to take a walk along Main Street and figure out what to take home for dinner," Elias said. "Want to join us?"

Her heart leaped. "I'd love to."

Nine

Elias led Tasha and Higgins across the street and onto the curb in front of the Huckleberry Inn. Despite Penelope Jones's actions these past months, Elias appreciated her care of the inn, aka the Crown Jewel of Berry Lake.

"Behold Main Street at night." The business lights and decorations were theme park-worthy. He hoped Tasha enjoyed seeing it as much as he did. "One of my favorite sights any time of the year, but December is extra special."

"I love everything. The lights. The decorations. The air even smells like Christmas." Tasha's head swiveled as she looked from one side of the street to the other, reminding him of someone seeing snow falling for the first time. "The town is so quaint, especially with the Christmas decorations. I thought Wishing Bay had the small-town quaintness factor wrapped up, but Berry Lake is a serious contender."

Elias stood taller. Despite his work issues, he couldn't wait to see his hometown through fresh eyes. "We can walk down this side, then grab a warm drink at Brew and Steep on our way to the park."

Tasha shimmied her shoulders. "Sounds like a plan."

Her excitement was infectious in the best possible way. She was, in a word, adorable.

As they passed the Huckleberry Inn, Tasha pointed to it. "That's the place to have breakfast, right?"

"Yes. I always order the aebleskiver."

"Oh, I've had those. When I skated at a competition in Denmark, I kept hearing about these little pancake balls. So good." She glanced from the inn to him. "Want to have breakfast there this weekend?"

"Yes." Elias didn't blurt the word, but it was close. Keeping himself from making a fist pump was easier thanks to a lesson learned during a mock trial competition in college. "Thanks to Higgins, I won't be going into the office on Saturday or Sunday."

"Do you usually?"

"Most weekends. But sometimes only for a couple of hours."

"Well, I'm glad fostering Higgins lets you have some free time."

"Me too."

Their gazes met. Locked.

Something shifted in Elias's chest. He'd better be careful if he didn't want to fall flat on his face. But that would be a small price to pay to focus all his attention on Tasha.

Higgins barked.

Tasha startled. "My Saturday will be full of practices for the ice show, but they don't start until ten."

"At the rink?"

"Not for the first ones. I'll be using the community room at the town hall."

"Higgins and I have to be at the rink when it opens. After that, I'll drop him at home and head over to help you."

"Higgins goes with you to the rink?"

"He hates being left alone." That was the only reason. If Elias could leave the dog at home, he would. "There's not much I can do during the week when I'm at work, other than spending my lunch hour with him, but I can let him tag along on weekends."

Her eyes twinkled. It must be the lights. "You like Higgins."

Elias's shrug was automatic. "What's not to like? He's a chill dog."

"Sounds like Sunday will be better than Saturday to have breakfast, then."

He nodded. "It's a date."

She rubbed her chin as if considering what he'd said. "A date."

"I'm looking forward to it." Even though she'd asked him to breakfast, Elias didn't want to send her running. "Love aebleskiver."

Her expression relaxed. "I'm ordering them too."

A date might've been pushing it, so Elias would be more careful with what he said.

As they continued strolling down Main Street, Higgins sniffed everything he could find, and Tasha's uncertainty seemed to disappear based on her smile.

"What are you thinking?" he asked.

"I can't believe I never thought to come to town at night."

"Now you know."

"And I'll be back." She glanced up at the sky. "Especially on nights like this."

"Clear skies make for colder weather."

"I'm an ice skater. I'm used to it." She released a contented-sounding sigh. "But Berry Lake…"

The way she practically sighed the words pleased him. "You like it."

"I don't like it." Her eyes sparkled, reflecting the lights. "I love it."

He knew she would away. The fact she'd remained in Wishing Bay after retiring suggested she was a small-town girl at heart. "Me too."

"Yet, you'd move?" Her tone was curious, but not in a stick-her-nose-in-his-business way, more like she was trying to understand.

"If I had to for my job." He'd been thinking about the possibility, but he'd never spoken the words aloud to anyone. "But moving doesn't mean I'll never return again."

"That's true." Tasha drew out the words as if thinking about them.

She seemed to have forgotten something. He would remind her. "You're considering the same thing."

Her lips parted, but she didn't say anything. She wet her lips. "Yes, I am," she said finally. "But other than my parents—and I bet they move closer to Alek and keep their house in Wishing Bay for weekends or vacations—nothing is holding me there other than sentimental memories." Her matter-of-fact voice told him she'd come to terms with leaving there. "It's beautiful on the coast, but this place…" She spun around with a whimsical smile. "It's magical. Have they filmed any movies here?"

"No movies, but there have been a couple Bigfoot TV shows." He pointed to the Sasquatch Adventure Tours. "The owner, Buddy Riggs, took film crews on overnight excursions to see if they could find Bigfoot."

"I saw nothing in the news. I assume the trips were a bust."

"Yep. They haven't found Bigfoot yet." Berry Lake would be known for more than the Bigfoot Seekers Gathering and Huckleberry Festival that occurred each summer if that ever happened. "Buddy has all kinds of tour packages. You can go out with guides for a few hours, the entire day, or overnight for however many days guests want. The packages range from roughing it to glamping."

She peered into the florist shop's window. "To find Bigfoot?"

"That's the goal."

The sweet melody of Tasha's laughter wrapped around and squeezed Elias's lonely heart. He wanted to hear her laugh again and again and again.

She rubbed her eyes. "That proves what my dad always says. People will spend their money on anything."

Forget money. Spending time with her was better than getting a full night's worth of sleep. She made him forget about everything except her.

"Have you gone out Bigfoot spotting?" Tasha asked.

Elias nodded. "It's a rite of passage in Berry Lake. There's even a program with the school district, but all I ended up with was an irritating case of poison oak."

"That must have been a bummer."

Funny, but she sounded almost disappointed. "I expected that, but on some nights, if you listen closely, you can hear Bigfoot call."

"For what?"

"A friend, family, pizza delivery."

Tasha shook her head. "And here I thought you were serious."

"I was kidding about the pizza." Elias raised his hand. "Scout's honor."

She side-eyed him. "How do I know you were a scout?"

Okay, she had a point. "If you search on Bigfoot shows and Berry Lake, click on any link that comes up, and you can hear for yourself."

"I'll do that when I get home." She stopped in front of the art gallery. The shop was closed, but lights illuminated the artwork on display in the front window. "That painting is like the ornaments at Charlene's."

He motioned to the placard sitting next to the oil painting of Berry Lake in the wintertime. "That's one of Hope Ryan Cooper's paintings."

"So talented. Someday, I want to own one of her works."

"The next time you're on Main Street, go inside the gallery if it's open. They have more of Hope's work on display. There's also a Bigfoot statue. A selfie with Squatchy is one of the town's top photo ops."

"I'll check it out. I'm here until the thirty-first, so plenty of time for a photo shoot. My brother and dad will get a kick out of it. Though Alek might know about Squatchy because of Logan Tremblay."

Elias met Logan through his wife, Selena, who'd grown up in Berry Lake and a client of the firms.

"You'll be here long enough to feel like a local by the time you head home."

"I hope so." Tasha tilted her head. "I like it here."

I like you.

Higgins barked. Nothing appeared to be there, but he ran around Tasha, and the tension from the leash pulled her toward Elias.

He caught her as she fell against him. "I've got you."

Her face—her mouth—was so close. The longing in her gaze made him come closer.

Higgins barked again.

Elias drew back. But he didn't want this moment to disappear. "Give me a minute, and then we'll continue this."

He unwrapped the leash from around them. Difficult to do with Higgins standing still and stiff like a statue with his tail sticking out and his ears perked. No other dogs were out. Maybe he'd seen a cat or raccoon.

A car passed them on the road, but Elias allowed the rest of the world to fall away as he focused on Tasha. "Now, where were we?"

As she stared through her eyelashes, his pulse took off. The corners of her mouth tipped up in a shy smile. "Right here."

"Yes, but I haven't asked you the important question yet."

"What's that?"

"Can I kiss you?" he asked.

"Please."

Elias lowered his mouth to hers. Warmth spread from the point of contact. She tasted like peppermint.

A Christmas kiss.

He would take it.

As his lips moved over hers, Elias wanted more than that first taste. He cupped the back of her head. He would have rather been touching her hair, but her cap was soft against his palm.

Next time, he would run his fingers through her hair.

There would be a next time.

One kiss would never be enough.

A catcall sounded.

Tasha stepped away. Her face appeared flushed, her breathing ragged.

Who needed streetlamps? His face must be beaming brightly. "Now, that's what I call a kiss."

She giggled, and he fell a little more for her.

"I agree." Tasha raised her chin. Her gaze sharpened. "But what are we doing here?"

"Standing in the cold and kissing."

"Yes, but what's going on with you and me?"

"Blame Higgins and his leash again." Elias didn't like the lines on her forehead or the ones surrounding her tight mouth. "You're only here until the thirty-first. That gives whatever this is an expiration date."

"So, something is happening."

"Most definitely, but we don't have to label it unless we want to."

"I'm not here that long."

"With me not knowing what'll happen come January, that's perfect. We can make the most your time in Berry Lake. And obviously, Higgins is crazy about you."

Her grin brightened her face. "Smartest dog in the world."

Any dog who not only brought Tasha into his life but also got them into a position to kiss deserved an extra bone and treat. "I agree."

They stood, staring at each other.

Higgins barked.

"I suppose he wants to keep walking." She sounded amused. "Too bad because I kind of like the floating vibe we've got going on."

His kiss made her float? Elias's chest puffed. "There will be more of that later."

Lots more.

As they walked, silence fell between them, but it wasn't an empty space that required words to keep things from being awkward. The quiet was comfortable and easy. So much so that he held her hand. She laced her fingers with his.

Even out in the cold, heat radiated through his chest.

They passed more shops—the windows brightly illuminated with miniature lights but the interiors dark.

Higgins scratched at the door of the Berry Lake Cupcake Shop.

"It's not open." Elias slowed to keep the leash from pulling too tightly. "Come on. I'm sure a barista will make you a treat too."

Higgins gave another scratch before rejoining them.

Cars drove along Main Street. Off in the distance, a siren sounded. The only place with customers coming in and out was Brew and Steep. None of that was unusual for Berry Lake. But Elias's complete disregard for anything but the woman next to him shocked him.

The sign for Brew and Steep reminded him of their plan. "Do you mind holding Higgins's leash? I'll go inside and order, and then you can go in to wait for the drinks and warm up."

"I don't mind at all." She took the leash. "Higgins and I became fast friends. I don't let just anyone climb all over me."

Lucky dog.

Higgins must've agreed, given the way he stared at Tasha as if she'd invented dog treats.

A short time later, they'd had a few minutes inside to warm up and hot drinks in hand. Higgins happily licked a small cup of whipped cream.

Elias held up his coffee. "A toast. To us making the most of our time together."

"It's not how I expected my vacation to go, but…" Tasha raised her hot chocolate. "Cheers."

He tapped his cup against hers and then drank.

This Christmas had the potential to rival the one when he got a new bike.

Tasha licked whipped cream from the side of her mouth.

Who knew? Elias sipped his coffee. This Christmas might even surpass that one. He sure hoped so.

Ten

The entire week passed in a blur, which was why each morning Tasha carved out time to skate on the lake alone. The overcast sky hinted at snowfall to come. That would make practices more challenging, but she would figure things out the way she had everything else. Elias's confidence in her must be rubbing off. She'd stopped second-guessing herself.

A little before noon, Tasha glided across the lake, enjoying the feel of the cold air on her face. Listening to the blade carve into the ice was one of her most favorite sounds in the world. The other was Elias's voice. She'd never realized how attractive a voice could be until she met him.

She dropped into a sit spin before continuing around the patch of ice she'd cleared with a broom. Not Zamboni smooth, but it worked. Like how things with Elias were working.

A romance hadn't been on her Christmas list. Who was she kidding? A date hadn't been on her radar screen.

But no regrets.

It wasn't like they saw each other *that* much.

She did a double Salchow.

With their schedules, they had to sneak in times to be together—usually a meal, though she'd watched a Christmas movie with him on Saturday. And she'd loved the aebleskiver almost as much as she enjoyed being with him. When they couldn't get together, a text or call sufficed.

If she were staying longer…

Nope.

She wouldn't go there.

Because she wouldn't stay longer. On December thirty-first, she would leave Berry Lake. And Elias hadn't minded her having a departure date. He appeared to consider that something positive. She did, too, if she were being realistic.

Tasha made a smaller circle and did a double flip.

Elias was nothing like her last boyfriend. Drew had been more than a guy she dated. He'd also been her skating partner, watching what she ate, telling her how to dress, talking over her in interviews. She'd gone along, wanting to do anything to make him happy, but that hadn't worked in the end. Male pairs skaters were like unicorns. Some acted like rock stars and got away with it. Of course, they did, given there were more females in need of a partner. In the end, he'd cared more about the Ramson name than she did. She'd been nothing but a wealthy skating partner.

Elias, however, treated her as an equal and with respect. They hadn't had any other deep conversations like the one over pizza, but this wasn't serious, so why should they?

Focus on the positives.

She did a spread eagle, one of her favorite elements, and then stopped to catch her breath.

Someone clapped.

Tasha glanced toward the shore to find Elias and Higgins standing there. She skated over to them. "What are you doing here?"

"I spent the morning at the county courthouse, so I swung by the house on the way home. Higgins wanted to come out here for a walk."

"Higgins, huh?"

"He may have had some guidance from his human GPS."

Tasha laughed. "I'm happy to see you. Does this mean we can have lunch together?"

"I have two egg salad sandwiches in the fridge and curly fries in the oven waiting for us at home."

Her stomach fluttered. The flutters had nothing to do with her favorite lunch food and everything to do with hearing Elias use *us* and *home* in the same sentence.

Uh-oh. That could be a problem.

Only if you let it be one.

Bottom line, on December thirty-first, she would say goodbye. Whatever they said or did would be over then.

Might as well enjoy being with Elias until then.

"If you're not finished skating, I can drop yours off at your place," he added.

"I'm ready to stop." She grabbed the skate guards from her sweatshirt pocket and placed them on the blades. "This might be the last meal I eat until later tonight."

"Practice?"

As soon as she stepped off the ice, Higgins greeted her. She patted him. "Yes. We're trying to squeeze them in between the public sessions."

"The kids looked great the other night."

"They're doing so well." Would the performance be flawless? Not a chance, but the kids would do their best, and that was all that mattered.

Sitting on a log, she removed her skates and put on her boots. "The kids keep improving. I'm thrilled with their progress. The high school choir director is working with the singers."

"I didn't know that. How did that happen?"

"Belle, who's playing the angel, and Gigi, one of the shepherds, asked him. It was as simple as that."

"That doesn't surprise me. Belle and Gigi are big fans of Selena's T and go for what they want."

Tasha stood. "Let's get lunch."

"Someone's hungry."

Tasha headed for the path. "Yes, and hangry me isn't a pretty sight."

Laughing, he followed her. "Guess this means I should bring you dinner."

Her heart stumbled. Better an internal organ than her feet. "Are you serious?"

He nodded once. "Do you want to choose, or should I surprise you?"

Tasha wasn't big on surprises because most never turned out well. But she trusted Elias. "Surprise me."

"Okay, I will."

Being with Elias was so easy. She stopped and faced him.

Higgins examined a tree.

Elias's forehead creased. "Something wrong?"

"No, everything's fine, but I want to say thank you. My December in Berry Lake would be much different if I didn't meet you."

"So would mine." He came closer. "And lonelier."

Tasha kissed him. The air was chilly, but he was warm and tasted like coffee. She wrapped her arms around him as if to remember this moment and this man.

You still have time left.

She wanted to savor every minute. And would.

* * *

The next night, as Tasha wrapped presents to give to the volunteers that have been helping at the practices, her cell phone rings with a FaceTime call from Alek. She accepted the call. "Nice hat trick."

Alek sat on his leather couch with an ice back on his knee. "Should've scored another one."

"You won."

"Could've won bigger." He brushed his fingers through his hair. "Are you still loving Berry Lake?"

She glanced around the cottage, but in her mind, she pictured the entire town. "Totally. This place is…special."

Alek snorted. "What's his name? If you can sneak a pic of his driver's license, I'll have a background check run on him."

Tasha froze. "What… What are you talking about?"

"I haven't seen that look in years, but I know it. That voice, too. You met someone."

Huh? "You asked me about Berry Lake?"

"Am I wrong?"

Tasha hesitated. "Phoebe is bringing me the skating costumes from the rink."

"You didn't answer my question."

"I met someone, but it's nothing serious." As soon as she spoke the words, they felt wrong. Whatever was happening with Elias felt like something. But she didn't want Alek to ask too many questions. "What about you? Have a new girlfriend du jour?"

He laughed. "Possibly, but I know it won't last. Never does."

"Who's fault is that?"

"Not mine."

She made a buzzer sound. "Wrong answer. It's one hundred percent your fault."

He shook his head. "Hockey, the lifestyle… it's too hard on relationships and marriage. Some of the teammates—"

"You're not them."

"Because I'm being smart about dating."

"And not settling down until after retirement," they said in unison.

She's heard the words so many times. "You're at the top of your game. That could be years from now."

Alek shrugged. "I'll still be a catch. So tell me about this guy…"

Ugh. Brothers!

* * *

Elias attended the next committee meeting without Tasha. She's been working so hard at the practices he knew she needed a break. Higgins sat at his feet as they listened to each of person give am update on their responsibilities.

"The Home for the Holidays program has resulted in four more adoptions. At this read, we'll break last year's record." Sabine looked directly at him. "Do you have anything to say about joining the ranks of foster failures, Elias?"

He stiffened but tried to remain cool even though sweat beaded at his hairline. "I enjoy having Higgins."

Higgins barked.

"I'm sure he'll find the right family to adopt him after Christmas," Elias continued.

Sabine frowned.

Penelope Jones grinned, not her usual look. "You're smart like your father, Elias. Dogs aren't right for everyone."

Sabine rolled her eyes. "Can you give us an update on the ice show, Elias?"

"Auditions went well. Skaters are learning their routines. Tasha has everything under control." He was so proud of her. "Did you have any specific questions?"

"How are ticket sales?" Penelope asked.

"They're picking up," he replied. "We're selling more each day."

And as word spread and the date drew closer, he had a feeling this would be their most successful fundraiser in Berry Lake history. He wanted that for his town but also for Tasha.

***

Before practice, Elias held onto Higgins leash walked next to Tasha. He wanted her to meet Grammy. They weren't officially dating, but he thought the two women would like each other. He motioned to the charming craftsman style house. Snow covered the front lawn. White Christmas lights hung from eaves. "This is where my grandparents live."

"Lovely home, but we don't have much time before practice."

"We won't stay long."

A Christmas welcome mat greeted them on the front porch. Elias rang the doorbell.

Elizabeth opened the door. Her gray hair pulled back into a braid, and she wore a red tracksuit that would make Mrs. Claus envious. A bright smile lit up her face. "What a wonderful surprise. You brought Higgins and a friend."

Higgins barked.

"Tasha, this is my grandmother, Elizabeth Carpenter." He smiled at Tasha before looking back at his grandmother. "Grammy, I want you to meet Tasha Ramson.

Tasha extended her arm. "Nice to meet you, Mrs. Carpenter."

"The pleasure is all mine. I've watched you skate for years. Knew you'd be a champion. Just wish you wouldn't have retired so young. You were an angel on ice."

Tasha shifted the weight between her feet as if uncomfortable. "Thank you."

"I should be thanking you for helping Elias with the ice show." Grammy opened the door wider. "Come in, come in. I baked cookies."

Higgins hurried inside. Tasha followed. Grammy gave him a curious gaze. "Take a seat in the living room. I'll grab the cookies from the kitchen."

"You're supposed to rest."

"Carrying a plate won't tired me out."

Elias sat next to Tasha on the couch. That was the only flat surface not covered with Christmas decorations. A tall tree sat in the corner. Four stockings, including one for Higgins, hang from the fireplace mantel.

Elizabeth carried in a plate of cookies and set it on the coffee. "If I didn't know you had practice, I'd make hot cocoa."

"A cookie will be great." Tasha took one and bit into it. "Delicious."

Grammy sat in the chair across from them. Higgins jumped onto her lap, and she giggled. "You're not supposed to be on the furniture, but we'll let that slide this once."

"Looks like you two attended the same dog obedience lessons," Tasha teased.

Grammy shrugged. "Pets like grandchildren are meant to be spoiled. Oh, wait. I don't have either to spoil unless you decide to adopt Higgins or get married."

Elias took a chocolate crinkle cookie. "Subtlety isn't a Carpenter strength."

Grammy giggled. "He isn't wrong. I worried the ice show would be too much for Elias, but now that you're here, everything will be perfect."

Tasha's cheeks turned pink. "I'll do my best."

Grammy nodded. "Of course you will. That's why you're a champion."

"Thanks." Tasha sounded almost shy, a way he wasn't used to seeing her. "I've been thinking of reaching out to some of the skaters I know. See if we can get a headline name to up ticket sales?"

"Ticket sales are on track, so you don't have to ask anyone," he said, not wanting her to think she wasn't lacking or something. Maybe he should tell compliment her. "You're doing a wonderful job."

Grammy nodded. "Enough about the extravaganza. Are you single?"

Elias shook his head.

Tasha laughed.

"What?" Grammy asked. "I want to get to know Tasha better. She isn't wearing a ring, but that doesn't mean there isn't someone in her life."

"I'm single," Tasha said without missing a beat.

"Interesting." Grammy leaned forward. "What about your hottie hockey player twin?"

Tasha coughed. She nearly dropped the cookie she held.

Elias cringed. His muscles bunched. This was not the direction he thought the conversation would go. "Grammy..."

Her hands flew up. "What? If I was sixty years younger..."

Tasha laughed, which made Elias relax slightly. "Alek is single too."

"Well, isn't that a coincidence. If you haven't guessed, Elias is single. Says he works too many hours to date. Isn't that ridiculous?"

Elias reached for another cookie. Chocolate chip this time. "Death by cookies sounds pretty good right now."

"No more cookies for you. I'm not doing the ice show alone." As she touched his arm to stop him, her gaze met his. Her hand lingered on him.

Higgins barked.

Elizabeth grinned as if Christmas had come early. "It's been great meeting you, Tasha. You and Elias and, of course, Higgins will have to come back and help me make more cookies, but you get to practice so you're not late."

* * *

Each day was better than the last. Despite nothing changing at work, Elias would have thought Christmas came early thanks to Tasha. He wasn't big on shopping, but he'd found the perfect present for Tasha. He couldn't wait to see her face when she opened the gift.

Okay, he wanted to see her all the time.

Elias loved being with her, and when they were apart, he didn't stop thinking about her. Even though they'd gone caroling with a group from the community church last night, he was counting the minutes until he could go to the rink and see her.

Focus.

Ugh. He sounded like Dad.

Still, Elias needed to finish up a few things.

He opened the document for Mrs. Vernon's living trust. She lived in a senior living center near her daughter. Both wanted to make sure all the legal paperwork was in order—it was—and to confirm Mrs. Vernon had enough money to remain in the facility long term. Elias had hired Bria Lawson, a CPA, to help with the second part, and he'd received her financial report that morning.

Elias reviewed the report and smiled. He would have good news when he spoke to her and her daughter tomorrow.

His phone rang, and he answered it. "Elias Carpenter with Carpenter Law Firm."

"I heard you're in charge of the outdoor rink."

A few reporters had contacted him about the rink and upcoming ice show. He hoped the media coverage brought in more money for the nonprofits. "I am."

"This is Drew Maddox." The guy's voice had an East Coast prep-school vibe. Old money. Stuck up.

The man wasn't one of the reporters who said they would call. "How can I help you, Drew?"

"Drew *Maddox*," the man repeated.

The name meant nothing to Elias. A quick search in his inbox showed nothing. "I'm sorry. I don't recognize the name. Have we met?"

Drew muttered something under his breath. "I'm a figure skater. Tasha Ramson and I go way back."

Elias ran an internet search on Drew Maddox. A photo of a blond-haired man and a woman competing at this year's Nationals appeared. Legit, but the guy looked like a preppy throwback from the eighties. Elias closed the tab on his computer.

"What can I do for you?" Elias asked.

"I heard about the ice show Tasha's putting on, and I want to help. My partner and I have some unexpected free time, and it looks like Berry Lake is only a four-hour drive from Seattle."

"Depending on weather or traffic. What kind of help?"

"Whatever you need. I'm that kind of guy."

And not humble. "Tasha mentioned reaching out to some skaters—"

"My partner and I are national champions."

And full of himself, but that was another matter. "Great. Tasha's the one in charge of the show."

"Yeah, right." Drew exhaled loudly. "But I thought it would be fun to surprise her."

Elias rubbed the back of his neck. Tasha enjoyed his surprise dinner from the Italian restaurant. He wished he'd taken a picture of the look on her face when he handed her the manicotti. "She might enjoy that."

"Oh, she will. Especially when she finds out my partner and I are happy to perform. Give your little show a name that audiences will be familiar with since Tasha's retired."

The words bristled. Elias didn't know if he was being hypersensitive, but something felt off. "Tasha isn't performing. Local teens and kids are."

"Just offering in case we could bring in more ticket sales. That *is* how you're raising money, correct?"

Drew had a point. "Yes, but Tasha has the final say in the show."

"Got it." Silence filled the line. "How about we show up for the dress rehearsal? Leave the rest up to Tasha."

Given there were still a few more days until then, Drew didn't sound as if he wanted to help that much. "Sure, but Tasha has the final say."

"I know. I know." Drew sounded frustrated. "See you then."

The line clicked.

Elias leaned back in his chair. That was an odd call. He should find out more about Drew Maddox.

Dad stormed into his office with papers in hand. "I need you to review these."

Great. More work. Elias straightened. "What are they?"

"Resumes."

He blinked. Not that anything with his vision would help his hearing. "What are they?"

Dad tossed the papers on the desk. "Resumes. Pick your top five for an associate and top ten for a paralegal. We may hire two more of those."

Elias nodded, unable to form a coherent sentence. Dad and Gramps had listened to him. Finally, they listened.

A weight lifted from Elias, making his arms and legs feel feather-light. He cleared his throat. "I'll have them for you tomorrow."

It would mean cutting his time short at the rink and with Tasha tonight, but…

"The day after is fine."

His jaw dropped. Literally. Dad had never given Elias extra time for anything. He pumped his fist under the table. "Consider it done."

Elias glanced at the time.

Go, clock, go.

He couldn't wait to tell Tasha about the firm hiring additional staff.

* * *

At the rink, Tasha stood in the middle with Belle and Gigi. It was getting late, and the temperature kept dropping. The other kids had gone home, but the girls had asked her to stay.

A handful of skaters circled the ice, trying to get the most out of the final session, which left the center of the ice free for them to work on Belle's sequence during the final piece.

"This is impossible." Belle threw up her arms. "I can't do it."

"You can," Gigi encouraged. "Isn't that right, Tasha?"

Tasha envied the two teenagers. Once upon a time, she and Kristen had been like these two young women. "Your best friend is right. You can do this. You've almost got the choreography."

"I feel a million miles away from where I need to be." Belle's breath hung in the air. "I'm trying. I really am. But I can't string the steps all together."

"Oh, I have an idea." Gigi bounced on her skates. "Tasha can skate the routine for you, and you follow behind her. That way you can get the timing because that's where you're having trouble."

Belle's timing was off, as Gigi said. But Tasha's stomach churned. A good thing she hadn't eaten dinner tonight. The idea of skating in front of these two made her want to throw up.

Pull yourself together.

Tasha cleared her throat. "Would following me be helpful?"

A stupid question because of course it would, but if Belle said no…

Belle nodded, tension seeping from her face. "Please?"

The hope in that one word shattered whatever excuses Tasha might come up with. Her skater needed Tasha to do this. It wasn't as if she would embarrass herself if she fell or made a mistake.

Still, her insides twisted one way and then another.

She glanced around. The couple who'd been skating had left the ice. So had two other people. Only the two teens, the volunteers in the rental trailer, and…

Elias.

When had he arrived?

He stood at the boards and waved.

Tasha waved back. He'd seen her skate. But skating in front of anyone else after what happened her first time there…

She would skate for Elias. Forget about everyone else.

Tasha swallowed. "Okay."

"Want me to play the music?" Gigi asked, her voice full of excitement.

"Yes, please." One deep breath followed another. The icy air stung, but Tasha hoped it numbed her nerves. She positioned herself a few feet in front of Belle and glanced over her shoulder. "Ready?"

"Yes."

The strains of "Angels We Have Heard on High" played. Tasha focused on Elias. She'd choreographed the routine out on the lake, but under the lights on the rink, she lost herself in the music.

Tasha flew across the ice. One stroke led into a jump. She landed and skated into the next move and then another. She nailed each jump and spin. And it was over.

Applause sounded.

"I did it!" Belle raised her hands in the air in victory. "Not as well as you, Tasha. But I figured out where I was making a mistake. Thank you."

Tasha's heart pounded. She tried to control her breathing. Not from exhaustion but exhilaration. Something she hadn't experienced in more than three years.

She smiled. "You're welcome."

Belle swayed as if she were skating the sequence in her head. "I want to try it again."

"Go ahead." Tasha left the girls and skated over to Elias. "Hey."

His bright gaze matched the smile on his face. "The way you skating. Amazing."

He hadn't looked that happy before. Tasha hoped she had something to do with his expression. "Thanks."

"No, seriously." Elias held her hand, raised it to his mouth, and kissed the top of her glove. "I'll admit I'm not a skating expert, but watching you skate takes my breath away."

"I appreciate it, but we're hanging out, so you have to say that."

He leaned into the board and kissed her hard, leaving her breathless.

"We're doing more than that." He brushed his lips over hers one more time. "But we decided not to label it."

"Right." Logically, they didn't need to, but her heart wanted to put a name on whatever this was.

"Tell your skaters it's time to go home because we're celebrating tonight."

"I thought you looked happy."

"I'm over the moon. If I knew how to dance a jig, I would, but I'll save you from that living nightmare."

She laughed. "You're practically giddy."

"I feel giddy." He laughed, and Tasha's heart wanted her to record the sound. "My father handed me a stack of resumes to review. They're hiring new staff."

Tasha shrieked. She threw her arms around his neck. "Yay! I'm thrilled for you."

He hugged her tightly. Being in his arms felt good, natural, where she belonged.

For now.

"Thanks." He leaned his forehead against hers.

"They haven't hired anyone yet, but I never imagined they would consider adding staff."

"This calls for a big celebration. Where do you want to go?"

"Home."

"Not out?"

He straightened, and she missed the contact with him. "I want to celebrate with you and Higgins by streaming a few Christmas episodes of *The Office*."

That gave her an idea. "We can pretend to be Pam and Jim."

"Do you want to be Pam or Jim?" he teased.

She laughed. "You *are* in a good mood."

Elias nodded. "Watching you skate was the buttercream frosting on the cupcake."

She hadn't heard that saying before. "Not a cherry on top?"

He laughed. "When you live in Berry Lake, it's always about cupcakes."

"Well, there are worse things than cupcakes."

"There's also something better." He kissed her forehead. "You."

Her heart thudded. Tasha had known falling for Elias would be easy. But until tonight, she didn't know how hard it would be *not* to fall in love with him.

What was she going to do?

Eleven

What am I doing here? A few days later, Tasha stood in Mrs. Carpenter's kitchen on the opposite side of the table Elias. Higgins ran all over the house exploring.

"I hope you enjoy baking, Tasha." Elias's grandmother wore a Christmas apron. "Each year, Berry Lake sponsors a giving tree, so people buy gifts for the families who are in need. A few of us prepare food baskets for them. These cookies will go in those."

Tasha didn't know Mrs. Carpenter well, but the woman was friendly and doted on both Elias and Higgins. "What a lovely tradition."

"It is." Mrs. Carpenter placed a cooling rack on the counter. "We're making the kind of cookies we can freeze. That way, I make them all month long, one type at a time, so there's a variety in the basket."

"Grammy's an expert cookie maker." The

affection in his eyes for the woman was clear and touched Tasha's heart."

Mrs. Carpenter winked. "My grandson is an expert cookie eater."

Tasha nodded. "I've seen that skill of his."

"Tasha bakes also," Elias added.

Elizabeth's eyes twinkled. She filled two bowls with ingredients and handed one to each of them to stir. "That's wonderful."

The baking continued with lots of laughter and some off-key singing of Christmas carols. Tasha couldn't remember the last time she'd bake with anyone. It must have been more than eight years ago at Kristen's house.

Elias stared at Tasha. "You have flour on your cheek."

Her hands were a mess. "Which one."

"I'll get it." He wiped her face with the side of her hand. "All gone."

Their gazes met. Lingered.

Tasha's pulse kicked up. "T-thank you."

He smiled softly. "You're welcome."

For some strange reason, neither of them seemed in any hurry to look away and break the contact. There seemed to be a connection between them as if a current of something flowed from him to her and back again.

Higgins barked, breaking the spell.

Elias glanced at the dog. "He wants a treat."

"No dough for dogs," Elizabeth warned. "Or humans."

As they made balls, Elias sneaked a taste of dough.

Tasha wagged her finger. "I saw that."

He held out dough to her. "Want some?"

"It'll make you sick."

Elias shook his head. "That's on old wives' tale so mom and grandmas get to eat all the dough themselves."

She laughed. "You sound like Alek."

He ate another bite. "Your brother must have excellent taste, too."

"I'm sure Alek Ramson is smart enough not to play chicken with salmonella," Mrs. Carpenter chastised before Tasha could. "Less eating and more baking or Elias won't be able to take you out for dinner."

That was news to Tasha. "Dinner?"

Elias shrugged. "Guess that's what my wingman wants."

"Your grandmother's your wingman?" Tasha asked.

"Her and Higgins."

Tasha shook her head. "I guess that's better than if it were Bigfoot."

"My dear." Mrs. Carpenter came closer. "You fit in perfectly in Berry Lake. I hope you consider extending your stay."

"I might." Tasha liked the town, but more

importantly she liked Elias. It might be worth staying and ringing in the new year with him.

* * *

Dinner turned out to be at a little café with linen-covered tables. A flickering votive candle and a single poinsettia flower in a vase sat off to one side of the table. Tasha sat across from Elias. It turned out Elizabeth had made them a reservation for two to say thank you for helping bake cookies.

Tasha enjoyed her entrée of salmon, asparagus, and rice pilaf. She set her fork on the plate. "Dinner was delicious. Thanks."

"I'm sorry for my grandmother less than subtle matchmaking efforts."

"That's what a wingman's for."

He laughed.

"It's sweet," she added.

Elias covered her hand with his. "I'm glad Grammy did what she did."

"Me, too." Tasha gazed into his eyes. "This vacation is turning into so much more than I imagined."

He squeezed her hand. "All good, I hope."

"The very best." She meant every word. "I'm having more fun with the ice show than I thought I would, too."

"Do you miss skating?"

"I skate every day. Sometimes more than once."

"I meant performing."

They'd already discussed competing and performing was different. "Sometimes. I loved the feeling when you know you've skated your best. People are on their feet cheering and clapping. Not because you'll score high for your country, but because they enjoyed what you just did for them. But…"

He leaned forward. "What?"

"My family wants me to skate again. Not Alek, unless I want to, which I don't. But my mom and dad…"

"Why don't you?"

"I skated pairs for a while. It wasn't the best partnership, either on or off the ice. It went downhill from there. I decided to skate on my own, but that worked out better for me. I didn't have to listen to someone blame me for making mistakes if we didn't do well. It was all on me. I preferred that."

"I'll be fully transparent and tell you I watched your routines at the Winter Games and Worlds. You're so talented. Why did you retire?"

"Skating lost its luster. But I do enjoy choreography and working on the show with you, so maybe I'll look into doing more of that." As long as Drew didn't mess it up again.

Elias sipped his water. "Depending on how the

show goes, I might remind you of saying that. If the town wants a repeat next year."

Tasha laughed. "Who wouldn't want to spend another Christmas in BerrLake? Though who knows where I'll be next year?

His gaze locked on hers. "Where do you want to be?

The answer hit fast and hard with a clarity she'd never experienced before. "Home."

Wherever that turned out to be.

* * *

Another week of practices and spending time with Elias flew by. She really liked him, and that scared her a little. Not as much as at first because he lived her and she lived… Well, that was what she was trying to figure out.

The ice show was coming together, and ticket sales seemed brisk. A good thing because no one Tasha had reached out to a few skaters she still had contact info for, but no one was able to come at this short notice.

A text notification buzzed on her cell phone. She glanced at the screen.

Mom: *What time will you be in Seattle on the 24th?*

Tasha groaned. Mom had been sending texts for

the past week, but more of the are you enjoying yourself or hope you're having fun type sentiments. But this…

Tasha typed on the screen.

Tasha: *I'm spending Christmas in Berry Lake.*
Tasha: *You and Dad will have a great time at Alek's. I sent presents for you to his apartment. It'll be like I'm there.*
Mom: *But you won't be there. I can't believe you won't come home. Is this about the rink?*

Tasha hesitated. Dare she be truthful? She thought about Elias finally telling his dad about hiring more help. Maybe she should do the same. She typed on the screen.

Tasha: *Partly. I lost my job, so I need to figure out what to do.*
Tasha: *But after being fired from the ice show in Seattle, I'd rather not be there.*
Mom: *We stay in Wishing Bay. You come home.*
Tasha: *Alek is expecting you in Seattle. He doesn't want to travel.*
Mom: *Then come to Seattle. If not for the parents who have worked to give you everything. Then for your twin brother.*

Tasha reread the exchange twice and lowered the phone. "At least I tried.

* * *

December twenty-second arrived in a blink-and-you-miss-it flash for Tasha. She hadn't remembered a time when the days sped by so fast. Then again, between the ice show and Elias, free time was at a premium. Not that she minded, but standing at the rink and holding a clipboard with the dress rehearsal's schedule, she had to laugh at what could only be described as controlled chaos.

Tasha didn't believe in Bigfoot—something she'd learned not to admit aloud in Berry Lake, where the invisible creature reigned supreme—but Santa might be real. At least his spirit. And that somehow, even though Christmas was three days away, he'd worked his magic because nothing else could explain how practicing for the show, having the right costumes arrive, and spending her free time with Elias had gone like clockwork when the odds should have been against that.

"Tasha, Tasha!" a boy, dressed as a sheep, yelled. "Am I supposed to say *baaa* while I skate?"

"You can if you want to." Elias had told her more than once that this was her show to run how she saw fit. She wanted the kids to have fun and look back on the experience with fond memories. If that meant making barnyard sounds, so be it.

She had a feeling he wouldn't mind. His giddiness

from the other night remained. He'd shown up at every practice since then and spent time with her afterward.

"Tasha, my mom wants to know when we'll be done." He spoke fast, barely pausing between words, and hadn't stopped moving.

She loved his excitement. It wasn't just him. The air buzzed with anticipation. Based on the jitters from the choir with their *Twelve Days of Christmas* sweatshirts and Santa hats, everyone at the rink was amped up and ready to go.

"I'm hoping in two hours." She glanced at her list. So much to get through tonight, but she'd experienced no nerves yet. Tomorrow night might—probably would—be a different story. "If not, we'll have someone text the parents we're running late."

"Thank you." The kid ran off.

She'd made the rule that only the volunteers and performers were allowed at the dress rehearsal, with one notable exception—Higgins.

For the past week, where Elias went, Higgins followed. That included their dates unless they ate out, but she didn't mind. The dog was so loveable, and he adored Elias as much as Tasha did. And don't get her started on their matching sweaters that Elias's grandmother bought him. He and Higgins were the cutest things ever. Elias also had mentioned nothing more about returning the dog on the twenty-sixth. Tasha hoped that was a good sign.

"Tasha, I need to go potty." A little girl in a snowman costume crossed her legs and squirmed. "I can't hold it much longer."

"Give me a sec." Tasha glanced around and found the perfect person to help. "Charlene, 9-1-1."

Charlene left her post with the eight kings and queens, formerly known as the wise men, and hurried over. "What do you need?"

Tasha tilted her head toward the wiggling snowman. "She needs to be taken to the restroom, please."

"Not a problem." Charlene motioned to the little girl, who had a worried expression. "Follow me, Frosty. You'll be smiling shortly."

Tasha reviewed her checklist. So far, so good.

Elias stood with the toy soldiers, who would perform the opening number to "March of the Tin Soldiers" from *The Nutcracker Suite*. There's been so many kids who wanted to be in the show the show's theme had been expanded beyond the original nativity idea.

Faithful Higgins, the unofficial mascot for the show, sat at his feet.

A young girl in a snowman costume came up to him. She was near tears. "My button popped off."

Tasha took a step toward them, but then Elias pulled something from his pocket. It looked like one of those small sewing kits, so she stopped.

"Want me to fix your costume?" he asked.

The girl sniffled. "Please."

Elias threaded a needle and sewed the button back onto the costume.

"Where'd you learn to sew?" the girl asked.

"My grandmother taught me." He tied off a knot and used the small scissors to cut the thread. "One button repaired."

The girl beamed. "Thank you."

She ran off to join the other snowmen. The guy was so good with kids. He'd make a great father someday.

Warmth rushed through Tasha. Her heart was in a puddle at her feet. She didn't have much time, but she needed to say something to Elias. "Hey."

He tucked everything back into the kit. "Big night."

"Until tomorrow. Thanks for helping with the costume."

"Grammy's sewing kit came in handy."

She glanced at the dog. "When are you adopting Higgins?"

Elias started. "I'm not."

Tasha didn't buy that for an instant. "The two of you are perfect together."

"He'd be the perfect dog for anyone. But I'm not right for him."

"Why?"

Elias glanced at the dog who was oblivious to the

conversation and more interested in all the kids around them. "Higgins needs more than a single guy. Look at how much he loves kids. He deserves to be adopted by a family."

She shook her head. "What he deserves is a forever home with someone who loves and understands him."

He shrugged. "We'll have to agree to disagree."

For now.

"You'd better get back to work," he said.

And Tasha did. She made her way to the group of kids by the entrance to the ice. She was grateful to Elias and the other volunteers Sabine had found. Enough that Tasha didn't have to worry about individual groups of performers. Still, there were so many pieces to coordinate that she was running on fumes and caffeine.

Only one more night to go!

Tasha inhaled deeply. She imagined the air in the North Pole held the same holiday joy she saw on the surrounding faces. That told her one thing. "This is going to turn out great."

"Now that I'm here, it will," a familiar voice rose above the chatter.

No. It couldn't be.

A shiver slithered down her spine, hissing when it reached her tailbone. The same tailbone she'd nearly broken when Drew had carelessly tossed her during a throw jump. She'd discovered later, he'd found a new partner, who was also his new girlfriend, even though he hadn't told Tasha.

She squared her shoulders and faced him. He was dressed as if he'd stepped off a photoshoot for an outdoor magazine, but his good looks were only a smokescreen to the devil within. With her blond hair and perfect cheekbones, Savannah stood with a bored expression as she stared at her phone.

Tasha's fingers tightened around the clipboard. "What are you doing here?"

Drew snickered. "Didn't Elias tell you?"

She flinched. How did Drew know Elias?

Her heart palpitated and her muscles twitched, reminding her of the last time nerves hit this hard. It had been more than three and a half years ago, going into the free skate in fifth place and needing the performance of a lifetime to win a medal at the winter games.

Stop. Tasha couldn't let Drew get to her. That was his MO. Somehow, he must have found out about her and Elias. They hadn't been keeping things secret.

She lifted her chin, not about to act demure in the way she once had. "Tell me what?"

"That Savannah and I are here to save the day. Or, in your case, the ice show."

His lofty tone had gotten more irritating over the years. It was worse than an earworm Tasha couldn't get out of her head. She wanted to gag. "As you can see, the day is fine. No saving required. You can go back to the hole where you came from and take your partner with you."

Drew tsked. "Not only partner. Fiancée."

As if on cue, Savannah held out her gloved left hand.

The news didn't surprise Tasha. What did surprise her was not caring at all. Talk about progress.

She stared down her nose at him. "X-ray vision isn't one of my superpowers. Now go."

His lips curled into a sinister smile. "Come on. Is that how you should speak to your headline act?"

Headline? Tasha stepped closer to get in his face. "The show is set. You're not part of it."

"Are you sure about that?" He feigned concern—something he'd disregarded for her.

"Positive."

"Well, Elias agreed you needed us to raise enough money for your cause and a bigger name would help the bottom line. You know I'm always willing to lend a hand." He made a fist, opened his hand, and spread his fingers. "Surprise! Here we are to bring in the big bucks."

Gigi screamed. "It's Drew Maddox and Savannah Savoy."

Kids surrounded the two, wanting to take photos and meet the pairs skaters. Drew and Savannah soaked up the attention like vampires who hadn't drunk blood in more than a hundred years.

Elias came up with Higgins on his heels. "What's going on?"

"Drew and Savannah are here!" Gigi stared at them with stars in her eyes. "Are they going to skate?"

A dreamy expression formed on Belle's face. "Can you imagine if we get to skate in the same show as them?"

As other kids piped in about wanting the pair to skate, Drew's expression grew smugger, and Tasha's muscles tightened until she thought one would rupture.

Elias clapped his gloves together. The sound was muted, but it got the kids' attention. "Everyone in place. The dress rehearsal is about to start."

The kids and teens reluctantly returned to their spots but not without looking at Drew and Savannah.

It was too good to last. Tasha should have known that. No matter what she did, Drew's mission was to stop her from achieving it. The worst part? She had no idea why.

Mom claimed jealousy. As Alek's star grew brighter, the media paid more attention to Tasha and less to Drew.

Could it be that simple and childish?

Knowing Drew, yes. He always had to have the spotlight. Her success as a solo skater must have annoyed him so much.

Tasha blew out a breath. She still had to figure out the connection between him and… "Elias—"

"Elias," Drew said a beat later.

He placed his hand on Elias's shoulder like an old friend would do, and something inside Tasha withered. It may have been her heart.

"Good to see you," Drew said. "I was telling Tasha how Savannah and I are happy to headline the ice show."

Elias's chin dipped. "I told you that was Tasha's call. She's in charge."

I told you.

The three words reverberated through Tasha.

I told you.

Drew hadn't been lying about speaking to Elias. Once again, she was the last to know.

I told you.

It had happened again. Her heart had rushed the take-off and under-rotated, ending up falling hard against the ice.

Splat.

Her breath hitched. Hot tears burned in her eyes, but this wasn't the place to show emotion. Not when everyone there was watching and listening. Tasha wouldn't drag this wonderful town of Berry Lake into her drama with Drew Maddox.

That meant Tasha was stuck.

Stuck holding herself in.

Stuck with Drew and Savannah.

Stuck not being able to find out what kind of game Elias was playing.

"What do you say, Tash-tash?" Drew knew she hated when he called her that. "You're going to put us in the show, right?"

Most people only saw the talented, charismatic Drew Maddox, not the controlling narcissist beneath the handsome façade. She would love to expose his ugliness and gaslighting habits, but this wasn't the time or place.

Unfortunately.

Tasha could tell them no, but the questions people would ask weren't ones she wanted to answer because that would require dredging up the past. She didn't want to do that. Oh, how she didn't want to bring that up ever again.

Pain at her temple sharpened and expanded to take over her entire head. Getting kicked with a toe pick would've hurt less. She massaged her temples.

It didn't help.

Drew scoffed. "She must be rearranging the numbers in her head."

Not even close. But no matter what had gone on between Elias and Drew, Tasha held the power for this show. She would wield it.

"You and Savannah can open the show," Tasha announced. "Give your music to the sound person. Hurry because you're on in five."

Drew's lower lip stuck out in an enormous pout. "We're not a warm-up act."

Tasha was through dealing with Drew. She glared at him. "Then you don't have to skate."

"But—"

"I'm not changing the order of the show." Her voice remained firm when her insides trembled. She glanced at her clipboard to compose herself. "Take it or leave it."

With that, she headed to the rink.

"Tasha," Elias called out. He ran after her. "I'm sorry. He said you were friends."

She stopped. "Drew's not a friend. Never has been. But I thought…"

"I told him you were in charge."

That didn't make her hurt less. All eyes were on them. "Not now. The dress rehearsal is starting. We can talk later."

Though she had only one thing she wanted to say to Elias.

Goodbye.

* * *

Molasses in January moved faster than how the time dragged during the dress rehearsal. Elias worked well under pressure, so no one could see inside he was a hot mess.

My fault.

He'd been so excited about Dad handing him the

resumes Elias had forgotten everything else, including doing more research on Drew Maddox. And that had hurt Tasha.

I've got to fix this.

But later.

Tasha was correct. The dress rehearsal was the priority. Plus, people would talk about Drew and Savannah skating as the warm-up act. Elias didn't want to fuel the gossip with lighter fluid, aka what was happening between him and Tasha.

Each act had a turn on the ice except for the choir, who sat behind the rink. There were a few wobbles, but that was show business, especially with kids involved.

Through it all, Tasha kept her cool. She didn't snap or frown or raise her voice once. However, she held her clipboard in front of her like a shield.

His respect for her kept growing, but so did something else.

Like, sure. Except he'd never felt this level of affection for anyone.

Higgins bumped against Elias's leg. "You don't count."

But I haven't known Tasha long enough to lo…

Pathetic.

Elias couldn't even say the word.

The choir sang a rousing version of "Twelve Days of Christmas," complete with hand movements to turn the song into an audience participation number. All the performers joined in.

Leave it to Tasha.

This would be the best holiday show Berry Lake ever had.

He only wished she didn't look so miserable. Oh, she smiled and encouraged the kids as she usually did. And if he hadn't seen her express genuine happiness, he wouldn't have known the difference.

But Elias had, and he did.

He tried focusing on the show, but all he saw was Tasha.

The last act prepared to go on the ice. Mary and Joseph and the manger animals skated out first. Next came the shepherds and angels. Belle nailed her solo. The kings and queens followed.

Not everyone skated well, and a few missed cues or lines, but that wasn't the point. The kids gave the same heartfelt performance they would have at a church or auditorium, but being outside, under the lights and stars, elevated the number.

As soon as practice ended, kids surrounded Drew and Savannah, who held court with patience and smiles. The two signed autographs and posed for photos, but Elias wanted them and everyone to disappear so he could talk to Tasha.

Apologize.

Kiss her worry away.

Finally, the rink cleared. Someone offered to buy Drew and Savannah dinner. And Tasha and the other volunteers appeared to have finished putting everything away for the night.

She walked toward Elias. "It's late. I'm cold. If you want to talk, come over. But I'm not doing it here."

"I'll drop off Higgins and come by."

His throat thickened, but some of the weight he'd been carrying tonight lifted. She hadn't slammed the door on him. That had to be a sign that things would be okay.

Thirty minutes later, he sat on her living room couch. She, however, sat across from him in a chair instead of next to him.

Not a good sign, but first things first. "I'm sorry."

She crossed her arms over her chest. "You apologized already."

Except it didn't appear to do much good. "I'm doing it again because I *am* sorry. I never wanted to hurt you."

"Then why didn't you tell me they were coming?" The pain in her voice matched the hurt in her eyes.

Elias leaned forward as if that would bridge the distance between them. He rubbed his sweaty palms on his pants. "You mentioned asking other skaters to perform to help with ticket sales. I thought Drew must be one of them, and he wanted to surprise you."

"I hate surprises."

He startled. That wasn't true. "You let me surprise you with dinner."

"Dinner is one kind of surprise." Her expression was neutral, but her voice trembled. "Having my ex-partner and boyfriend show up with his latest partner-now-fiancée to skate in the ice show I've been asked to help run is another."

Elias let out the breath he'd been holding. He dragged his hand through his hair. "I had no idea."

"Obviously." Her tone, however, wasn't snarky. She leaned forward. "I suppose you also didn't know that while I was recovering from an injury that he caused announced he had found a new partner before telling me. Or that he spread lies about me, ones that kept getting worse the more success I had without him. And he's the one who got me fired from the ice show."

Elias's face paled. "I swear. I had no idea any of that happened."

Tasha eyed him warily. "Aren't lawyers good at research?"

"I searched to make sure he was legit." Elias wouldn't make excuses for himself. "I meant to follow up, but something came up, and I forgot to continue."

"He said you agreed we needed a headliner."

"You're the one who said other skaters might help ticket sales. The guy told me he wanted to help. What he said made sense."

"If Drew and Savannah were here to help boost ticket sales, why weren't they added to the flyers or social media posts? Keeping them as a surprise makes no sense if more sales was the goal."

Tasha was right. "It's not an excuse. But I thought he knew you better than me."

"Neither of you know me at all."

Elias flinched as if he'd been sucker punched. "That's not true."

Her gaze didn't waver. "If it were, you'd understand Drew Maddox is the last person I'd ever want to see."

"You never told me what happened."

"Might have to work on your cross-examination skills, counselor, because you never asked."

She was slipping away, but Elias didn't want to let her go. "I've apologized. Let me make this right."

"There's nothing for you to do."

He sucked in a breath.

"This thing between us was always going to end," she said in a matter-of-fact tone. "We're just ending early."

Elias felt as if he were falling. He gripped the sofa cushion for support. "You don't leave until the thirty-first. Let's hang out until—"

"I can't." Her voice cracked, and her mask slipped, leaving hurt-filled eyes and a sad face.

He hated seeing her hurting. "I'm not ready to say goodbye."

"I am." Her eyes gleamed with unshed tears. "I need to do this for me. The same thing keeps happening. I'm always the last to find out things, even when I'm the most affected by what's happening. It happened with Drew multiple times. My friend Kristen. Even my parents. It's a pattern I must break. I thought you were different."

"I am." The words shot out. "I made a mistake. I was only trying to do what was best for the ice show to raise money. That shouldn't ruin things between us."

"Maybe not for you, but for me, it ruins everything." Tasha rubbed her eyes. "I still need your help at the performance tomorrow night."

"Of course. I'll be there. I'm not giving up on you and me."

"I'm leaving soon." Tasha wouldn't meet his eyes. "You'll get over it."

No, he wouldn't. But she wasn't in a place to hear that.

He stood. "I'll be there tomorrow night, but I hope you decide you want to fight for us too. Because I can't do it on my own. Good night, Tasha."

* * *

If Tasha was lucky, she might have slept three hours last night. But Elias had been on her mind, whether her eyes were open or closed. He'd looked so sad, so resigned when he'd left the cottage. But no matter how tired or upset she was, she wouldn't let the kids down, which was why she'd bought an oversized cup of coffee from Brew and Steep and brought it with her to the performance.

Now at the rink, the energy was higher than last night. Bleachers had arrived and additional lighting too. Charlene and Juliet had used their event-planning skills to decorate the park even more. Shops and restaurants had set up booths using pop-up tents. They sold everything from coffee to cupcakes.

It was, in a word, spectacular.

But a weight bore down on Tasha.

Later, she imagined Mom saying. *The performance comes first.*

Tasha agreed. She would gladly exchange her mittens for boxing gloves. Drew Maddox had stolen too much from her. She would put up a fight if he tried to take this show too.

As the kids arrived, the bleachers filled with parents and others.

Phoebe McAllister hugged Tasha from behind and whispered in her ear. "You look exhausted."

"I am. And a little heartbroken."

"The hunky lawyer?"

Tasha nodded. "He knew Drew and Savannah were coming."

Phoebe cringed. "Ouch. I'm sorry, but remember, everyone makes mistakes. Many are unintentional, even if they hurt."

"Elias didn't know about my past with Drew. But

I'm tired of hurting. Of always being the last one to know. Of paying the price for only wanting to help."

Phoebe touched Tasha's shoulder. "I don't blame you, but don't lump everyone into the same bowl."

"Elias agreed about us needing a headline act. He didn't believe in me."

"Where did he get the idea of inviting other skaters?"

"Me." As realization hit, she stared at the floor. "Which means I'm the one to blame for all this, but I took it out on him last night."

"Look at me."

Tasha did.

Phoebe's gaze met hers. "Why'd you do that?"

All the voices from her past swirled in Tasha's head. Images and words. Hurt and betrayal. "No one's believed in me. How do I believe in myself? I thought Elias was different. I wanted him to be different. Finding out he kept Drew coming from me…"

"Hurt you. I understand." Phoebe's voice was soft. "But just so you know. Alek believes in you. He always has. So do I."

Tasha's eyes stung. She blinked.

Phoebe moved them off to the side where they had more privacy. "You're one of the most talented skaters who's blades ever touched the ice. But the one thing missing has been self-confidence. You've listened to what everyone else said. You tried to be whatever they wanted. It wasn't until you wouldn't let your mom push you into another pairs partnership that your skating career soared."

Tasha nearly laughed. "I forgot how badly we argued over that."

"I can see why you'd want to forget it."

She sighed. "I guess I just thought I was over everything that happened in the past. That I'd put it behind me."

"You mean Drew?"

"Drew and Kristen."

A beat passed and another. Phoebe rubbed her neck. "Kristen was heartbroken over Alek."

"What happened between them had nothing to do with me. She was like a sister to me. She was the only one who knew…"

"Knew what?"

Knew the truth about how badly Drew treated Tasha. When he'd dumped her, she'd had no one to talk to. If she'd told Alek the whole truth, he would have hurt Drew and maybe himself in the process.

She swallowed. "Nothing."

Phoebe's expression was compassionate as if she understood. "I told Kristen cutting you off was a mistake, but she decided to go no contact with anyone that reminded her of Alek for her own sake. It never had to do with you."

"It sure felt that way. I've tried…"

"You have but keep trying. It's never too late."

She wasn't sure about that.

Phoebe touched her shoulder. "I know you came to Berry Lake to figure out what comes next, but maybe you should figure out you."

Tasha flinched. "Me?"

"You've been in the spotlight since you were born. You've always been aware of what others think of you and their expectations for you. Both people you know and strangers. Even after you retired."

Tasha hated how much that was true. "Direct hit."

"Sorry, not sorry. But I want you to try to one thing for me."

"What?" Tasha asked.

"Believe in yourself. Trust yourself. Love yourself. Once you do, everything will fall into place."

If only… "You make it sound easy."

"It's not. But trust me, it's doable." Phoebe smiled softly. "I booked a room at the Huckleberry Inn. I'm here to support you with the show and with whatever else you need. I'm not driving home until tomorrow."

Affection for Phoebe rushed through Tasha. More than once, she'd wished the woman had been her mom. She hadn't gone so far to throw a piece of sea glass in the bay, because she loved her parents, but she'd considered it. "Thanks. I'm happy you're here. I didn't tell my parents I was helping with this show."

"That's understandable." Phoebe glanced around.

"Yelena would have been all over the performance."

That brought a laugh. "You're right. I love her, but I wish Mom were more a mother than a coach. I had plenty of coaches but only one of her."

"Never doubt her love for you and your brother."

"I know, even if she has a strange way of showing it."

"She grew up in another country, in another time. She had to succeed to survive. Skating defined her, and she put that same pressure on you."

"Thank you." Tasha needed to focus on the present, not the past. "Can I say how great it is to see you here? Thank you for driving all this way to see our ice show."

"I'm thrilled to be here. Berry Lake is a cute town. And since there's no longer a rink and show in Wishing Bay, I figured this was the best option." Phoebe hugged her. "Now, chin up. Show these landlocked folks what beach peeps are capable of."

"Will do."

"Tasha." A haggard-sounding Gigi ran up. She wore her costume and held a dress bag. "This is bad. Really bad. Terrible."

"Slow down and breathe," Tasha said. "Then you can tell me what's wrong."

A few people had come closer after seeing Gigi running up. They weren't Tasha's concern. She focused on Gigi. "Better?"

"Yes." Gigi took another breath. "Except Belle has the stomach flu. She can't stop throwing up. She won't be here tonight, but I have her costume for someone else."

"Oh, no. We're missing the lead angel." Katie's voice cracked. Other kids chimed in with their woes.

"Savannah can be the angel, and I'll be her shadow." Drew reached for the dress bag.

Gigi wouldn't let him have it. "The costume won't fit you. Savannah is shorter than Belle, who's the same height as…" Gigi stared at Tasha. "You should be the angel. You knows the routine, and the costume will fit her."

Phoebe nodded. "If it doesn't, there's someone in the audience who can help with that."

Tasha's heart lodged in her throat. "Kristen's here?"

"She didn't want me to drive alone." Phoebe winked. "But that was only her excuse to be here."

Drew rolled his eyes. "Who cares? Tasha retired. She can't skate."

"Yes, she can." Gigi handed the dress bag to Tasha. "Please. Belle feels like she let everyone down. You're the best person to take her place."

"It'll ruin the show," Drew said under his breath.

"Drew, stay here." Tasha looked at the kids. "Don't worry. Everything will be fine. Go get in place."

They did.

Drew reached out his hand. "Hand over the costume."

Tasha had stayed quiet long enough. She wouldn't take this any longer. She held the dress bag behind her. "No. You and Savannah are skating the opening number, and that's it. You've done everything you can to ruin me, but no longer. If you cause any more trouble in my life, I'll write a memoir that'll rock the skating world and destroy yours."

He flinched. "I—"

"I have receipts. Texts, emails, and voice mails. I may have taped a few conversations too."

His face dropped. "You wouldn't."

She raised her chin. "Try me."

Drew opened his mouth and then closed it, but his eyes shot killer laser beams at her. He grabbed Savannah's hand. "We have to get ready for our skate."

With that, they stomped away.

Phoebe applauded. "Way to go, Tasha."

"I'm impressed." Elias joined them. "I see why you hate Drew."

"I don't hate him." Once, Tasha had. But no longer. "That would mean I cared for him. I'm…indifferent. I feel sorry for him and Savannah."

Tasha should make sure the skater was okay.

"I'll give Sam a heads-up to watch the guy."

"Thanks." She didn't know what else to say.

Elias motioned to the dress bag. "You'll make a beautiful angel."

"Thanks." Skating was the last thing she wanted to do, but she would do it. For Belle and the other kids, but also for herself. As Phoebe had told Tasha, she needed to believe in herself.

"Break a leg." Phoebe hugged her. "Text if you need Kristen to help with the costume."

"Thanks." Tasha stared at Elias. "And thank you for being here tonight."

"I have to get over to the tin soldiers, but I…" He wiped his face. "If you get nervous—not saying you will—but if you do, just remember, you've poured your heart into this show. Your skating will blow everyone away."

Tasha clutched the dress bag. "Thank you."

He nodded. "See you around."

If only… She sighed.

*   *   *

The show started shakily. As Elias watched from the side, Drew and Savannah made mistakes and fell twice. The audience, whether or not they followed skating, could tell something was off with the pair. But each act after that did a fabulous job. Not perfect, but perfectly entertaining. The smiles on the audience members' faces and applause told him he wasn't the only one with that opinion.

When the final number started, Elias's heart wanted to explode out of his chest. As Tasha skated onto the ice, he held his breath. She was the perfect angel.

His angel.

He wanted her to be his, but how?

Twelve

The final strains of "Angels We Have Heard on High" played. Instead of a single spin, she did a combination spin ending with the Biellmann, a layback variation with her legs in almost a full split.

She came to a stop.

The applause went from her ears to her heart.

I did it!

Tasha joined the choir of angels to finish the nativity number. And when that ended, the crowd rose to their feet.

The kids stared in awe. Tasha felt the same way.

She directed the curtain calls on the ice, and the show was over. People were leaving. Volunteers packed up, and she still had her skates on.

"This is for you, Tasha." Katie handed her a Christmas present. "Thanks for doing the show. Performing was so fun."

"You were an excellent Mary." Tasha hadn't expected a gift. "Thank you for being a part of it."

More kids dropped off presents until she could no longer hold them all in her arms. She couldn't believe at the generosity of everyone. A part of her felt as if she belonged there, something she hadn't felt in a long time.

"Let me help you." Phoebe held a box. "A certain hunky lawyer thought you might need this."

"That was thoughtful of him." Tasha didn't check to see if he was there.

Kristen took the presents from Tasha's arms and put them into the big box. "Lots of gifts to open on Christmas morning."

Tasha forced a smile. "Yes."

"You need to go home and sleep." Phoebe gave her a mom-look. "We're having breakfast at the inn. Please join us. Say nine o'clock?"

Tasha wanted to say *yes*, but she glanced at Kristen first.

Kristen appeared sheepish. "I'd like for you to join us."

Tasha sucked in a breath. "Are you sure?"

As Kristen's eyes gleamed, she nodded. "Please. I'd love to catch up. And Mom's a good referee if it comes to that."

Phoebe beamed. "I am, but I also know when to let things play out on their own."

Tasha had nothing to lose, right. "Sure. I'll be there."

* * *

The next morning, Tasha entered The Huckleberry Inn. Instrumental Christmas music greeted her. The interior of the Victorian was decorated from top to bottom. The large foyer which doubled as a lobby contained a Christmas tree. A lighted garland hung from the front desk.

A sign pointed to the dining room.

She didn't know if Phoebe and Kristen were already seated or if Tasha had been the first to arrive. She took a step in that direction to see Savannah walking toward her.

Savannah held a cup of coffee and an orange. "Do you have a minute?"

Tasha had no idea what the woman would want to talk to her about. They'd never been friends, and the skater had kept her distance when she became Drew's partner. "I'm meeting Kristen McCallister and her mother for breakfast."

"I saw them in the dining room." Kristen had competed at the regional level so would know Savannah, who glanced over her shoulder as if double checking. "It won't take long."

Tasha wanted to get this over with as quickly as possible. "Go ahead."

"I didn't see you after the show. Drew wanted to get out of there."

Tasha thought that was understandable, given what had happened.

"I wanted you to know you skated beautifully last night," Savannah continued with an unexpected compliment. "And I'm sorry what happened with the ice show in Seattle. Drew used me as the excuse to get you fired, but it wasn't me. I wanted you to know."

Tasha wasn't sure what to sway. "Um, thanks."

"You should keep skating. Drew…"

A closer look at Savannah showed bags under her eyes and her face was haggard without all the makeup she'd worn at the dress rehearsal and show. She also was thin. "Are you okay?"

"I'm fine." The words rushed out. "Hungry."

Huh? Savannah had been coming out of the dining room. "Didn't you eat breakfast?"

Savannah glanced at the orange but said nothing.

Warning lights flashed. "When I skated with Drew, he was always on me about my weight. No matter how much I lost, he claimed I was too heavy."

Savannah's wide eyes locked on hers. Tasha knew she had to speak up. Even though she had spoken to Drew, the guy could be pulling the same stunts with his current partner, who was also his fiancée. At one point, Tasha had been the guy's girlfriend.

"I did everything I could to lose weight," Tasha

admitted. "Sometimes, I didn't eat enough. It wasn't healthy, and it effected my ability to perform at the level I needed to. You're a world-class athlete. You need protein and carbs. You're in perfect shape. Don't let him tell you differently."

Savannah bit her lip.

"Other things that happened with Drew made me doubt my abilities and myself," Tasha added. "I was so young."

"A teenager," Savannah whispered.

"Only a couple years younger than you when you became Drew's partner."

They were adults now. But age wouldn't stop the abuse of a spoiled narcissist like Drew. "I didn't know better, then. I do now. If you ever need to talk or help, whatever, please let me know."

"You'd want to talk to me? Help me?" Savannah sounded shock. "After everything that happened?"

"I'm guessing your parents had a bigger role in Drew becoming your partner than you did. And you weren't the reason he wanted to stop skating with me." Savannah's dad had probably bought the best partner he could for her daughter.

Savannah glanced around. Was she looking for Drew?

"I wish I didn't love him so much." Savannah's expression was bittersweet. "Sometimes I think things would be better if we didn't skate together."

"That's what I thought too." Remembering the throw gone wrong, Tasha rubbed her hip. "Be careful telling him that."

"He's not as bad as he was with you." Savannah was quick to defend him. "He admitted he made some mistakes."

Some. Wasn't that rich? Tasha forced herself not to laugh. "Get more to eat. And call me if you need an ear."

Or a shoulder.

With that, she entered the dining room and made her way to Phoebe and Kristen, who sat at a table near the window. She sat next to Phoebe. "Good morning."

"Were you talking to Savannah?" Phoebe asked, curiosity in her eyes.

Tasha placed her napkin on her lap. "Yes."

Kristen made a face. "Is Drew pulling the same stuff with her?"

"I don't know." Tasha glanced at the doorway to the dining room. Savannah hadn't returned to get more food. "Maybe."

Lines creased Phoebe's forehead. "What stuff?"

Tasha took a sip from the glass of water at her place setting. Only Kristen knew everything Drew had done, and when she'd walked away from their friendship, Tasha had been left with no one to turn to for help. "Skating things."

Kristen bit her lip. She shifted in her seat. "I'm so

sorry, Tash. I treated you no differently than Drew did. You deserved better."

"I did."

Phoebe flinched, but to her credit, she didn't say anything. Instead, she sipped her coffee.

"You did, but I only thought of myself. I was so hurt when Alek told me he didn't want to be friends or part of my life any longer."

"That was as much my parents as him."

"I know, but you—"

"We were best friends." Tasha stared into Kristen's eyes. "You pushed me out of your life like I was some stranger, not a sister from another mother."

Kristen's eyes gleamed. "I was so selfish. I wasn't thinking of you as my friend. Only you as his twin sister. I didn't want anything that reminded me of him."

"Do you know how that made me feel?" Tasha sniffled. "Especially when my life started falling apart with Drew. No one else knew…"

"I'm sorry. I responded the only way I could. I'm sorry you paid the price. I know we can't go back, but maybe we can try to go forward."

Silence filled the table.

A server came up and took their orders. When she left, Phoebe patted Tasha's hand. "There's a lot of water under the bridge. A decision doesn't have to be made today, but I'm happy the two of you are talking."

"I never stopped talking," Tasha blurted. "Or trying to talk, even on the last day the rink was open."

"If you want me to feel even guiltier, you're succeeding." Kristen sipped her coffee. "When you get back to Wishing Bay, I hope you'll try again. Because this time, so will I."

Tasha nodded, except a part of her didn't want to return to Wishing Bay. She couldn't stay in Berry Lake, though. So where did that leave her?

* * *

On Christmas Eve, Elias and Higgins sat on the floor in his grandparents' living room. Logs crackled in the fireplace. A plate of homemade cookies sat next to cups of eggnog on the coffee table. A Christmas movie played on the TV. It was the same as every other December twenty-fourth, but something was missing.

Not something.

Someone.

Tasha.

Elias sighed.

Higgins wiggled, his sign that he wanted rubs.

"You've spoiled that dog," Dad said from the couch.

Grammy clucked her tongue. "Pets are meant to be spoiled. The same as children."

Gramps harrumphed. "Elias is the least spoiled child I know."

"That's because you know how wouldn't let us spoil him." Sounding affronted, she pointed at Dad. "At least I was allowed to bake for him when he was growing up."

"You spoiled me enough. Still do." Elias didn't want her to get upset with her heart condition. "And you know I'd rather have your cookies than anything."

At the sound of "cookies," Higgins jumped to his feet.

Elias laughed. "Higgins agrees."

"Thank you." Gratitude shone in Grammy's eyes. "Are you keeping him?"

"I'm thinking about it." Which surprised even Elias. "He's a good boy and seems to be okay with my schedule."

"You don't have time for a dog." Dad grabbed a cookie. "You should find a girlfriend first."

"My grandson is a catch." Grammy picked up her eggnog. "When he's ready for a relationship, I'm sure Higgins might help him find a girlfriend or a wife."

Elias remained silent. He focused on the movie, but the image on the screen blurred. Higgins had already found him the perfect woman. Elias needed a plan to get her back. It was only the twenty-fourth. She wasn't leaving until the thirty-first. He had time to come up with something.

* * *

On Christmas morning, Elias sits next to the tree with Higgins. They wore matching their Christmas sweaters. Ripped wrapping paper was all over floor. There were enough dog toys for an entire rescue, but one present remained beneath the branches.

Elias pointed at it. "Looks like there's on left, bud. It's from Santa Paws."

He pulled the gift closer and helped Higgins open it. "Look. It's a cushy dog pillow with your name embroidered on the front."

Higgins sniffed the pillow. His tail wagged.

Elias placed the pillow in the dog's favorite spot next to the fireplace. "Look at that. Your pillow fits perfectly."

As Higgins spun around, Elias went to the front window. Snow fell. He glanced toward cottage and sighed. He wished Tasha could see how perfectly they could fit together, but that might take a Christmas miracle.

* * *

On Christmas morning, Tasha woke up shivering. She opened her eyes. The smell of vanilla and cinnamon were familiar, but the beamed ceiling wasn't her usual morning view.

She bolted upright.

What was she doing on the living room couch? With the lights on?

Her gaze zeroed in on the cupcake liners and crumbs on the coffee table.

Drowning her sadness in sugar must have worked. Her jeans would fit tighter, but she didn't care. The dark cloud still hovered above her, but she breathed easier. Her eyes no longer stung and burned, though they felt puffy and achy from crying.

Not to say she wouldn't cry later—she likely would.

Tasha wasn't okay, not by a long shot, but she was…better. A bruised heart and dashed hopes wouldn't stop her. No matter how much she hurt or how long it took to get over Elias, she would survive the same way she'd survived everything else.

Only this time, she would come out stronger.

Of that, she had no doubt.

Tasha Ramson wasn't the same person who'd arrived in Berry Lake earlier this month. That much had been clear after how she'd dealt with Mom, Drew, Savannah, and Kristen. Tasha had come to Berry Lake to figure out what she wanted to do next. What she'd really needed to do was stand up for herself. Ignoring what happened, remaining silent, trying to avoid conflict were why she'd been stuck. It was all her. But no longer. She could stand up for herself when she needed to and forgive when necessary.

She blew out a breath. Elias had given Tasha so much, and even though things hadn't worked out, she had zero regrets. Whatever she did. Wherever she ended up, Tasha would be okay. And when her heart healed, she would be ready to find love again.

Somewhere out there was the place she belonged, where she would thrive and be loved for whom she was. A part of her had hoped that would be there in Berry Lake, but she would find another.

The lights on the tree glowed festive and bright, a beacon for her future. Thank goodness she'd never asked for the tree to be taken down. She would have missed it.

A part of her wished her family were there, but she'd made the right decision to spend the holidays without them. Still, she hugged herself the way Mom and Dad would if they were with her this morning. "Merry Christmas."

Speaking of which… Tasha jerked around to peer outside. Snow fell—lots and lots of snow.

She scrambled, kneeling backward on the couch to see better. At least three new inches had fallen.

Yes!

Tasha touched the windowpane. The glass was smooth and cold against her palm. Even though Berry Lake had been covered in white the entire time she'd been there, seeing the snow made the day more special. "A white Christmas."

Exactly what she'd wanted. A broken heart hadn't been on her Christmas list, so it didn't count.

After she made a pot of coffee, Tasha showered. Once she was dressed, she put cinnamon rolls—the kind that came in a tube—in the oven. It wasn't long before she placed a cup of coffee and a plate with two cinnamon rolls on the coffee table. She turned on the gas fireplace, so flames danced and added some warmth beyond the heat, and she clicked the playlist of carols on her cell phone. The sounds of Whitney Houston's "Do You Hear What I Hear" filled the living room.

"Now, it's time to celebrate Christmas."

With her breakfast within arm's reach, Tasha sat on the floor in front of the tree. Small gifts from kids in the show sat under the branches. She'd been so surprised when so many gave her a thank-you present.

She reached for two cards. One from her parents and the other from her brother. They would ask if she'd opened theirs when they called.

The one with her name scribbled in barely readable handwriting was from Alek. She opened that one first.

A thousand-dollar Visa gift card and a gift certificate for three personal development sessions with Selena T, the wife of his teammate with a hit podcast.

Alek might be so wrapped up in hockey that she didn't see him much, but he'd always been generous, even as a kid. And Tasha was interested to see what the famous life coach had to say. Maybe she would get some direction.

Next was the envelope with Mom's perfect handwriting. Tasha opened the card and gasped at the ten-thousand-dollar check inside. The amount shouldn't surprise her. Mom spent that much on a purse, but Tasha read the memo line aloud.

"Tasha's fresh start."

A lump formed in her throat, and the place behind her eyelids grew hot. She had a little in savings but not enough to cover deposits when she moved.

When not if.

She blinked and reached for a rectangular box wrapped in candy cane-striped paper and tied with a red satin ribbon. The tag said it was from Jett, who'd played Joseph. She unwrapped the gift to find a box of chocolates shaped like ice skates. "Those are so cute."

A quick photoshoot happened on the coffee table using wrapping paper and ribbon as a backdrop.

The next present came in a Santa gift bag with red and green tissue paper sticking out of the top.

Her phone rang. *Mom* illuminated the screen. Tasha accepted the call. "Merry Christmas, Mama."

Mom was dressed with a full face of flawless makeup, as usual. "Merry Christmas to you, *moya solnishka*. How are you?"

"I just opened your present," Tasha said. "Thank you for the check."

"Is nothing."

"It's everything." Tasha knew they wouldn't miss the money. "I'd like to make a fresh start somewhere."

"Would be nice if you and Alek were in the same town, yes?"

Tasha laughed. "We'll see."

"Hey, sis." Alek appeared on the screen. "You know you're more than welcome to one of my guest bedrooms. You can stay as long as you want to. Think high-rise penthouse condo with all the amenities, including a concierge."

Tasha laughed. "I've been there, bro."

"Oh, right." He laughed. "No excuse but to stay with me. Spend a couple of months seeing if you like Seattle."

Funny, he almost sounded serious. "Did Mom and Dad put you up to this?"

"Absolutely…not."

"So just Mom."

He laughed. "Guess I didn't get all the brains in this family, but it's a solid plan. This place is too much for just me."

The idea had merit, but… "Living with your sister might cramp your style."

He snickered. "My style is so on point nothing can cramp it, including you."

Tasha rolled her eyes. "Modest as ever."

"As humble as a hat trick," he joked.

"I'll think about it. And before I forget, thanks for the sessions with Selena T and the gift card."

"Don't spend it all in one place," he teased.

"Is speaking in clichés part of your hockey training?"

"It's called giving soundbites."

"You could try to sound less—"

"Clichéd?"

"Yes." Alek might be an all-star hockey player, but he was smart enough to get into two Ivies back east. "But if it works for you…"

"It does." He sounded like he was smiling. "Lovely ladies are lining up to date me."

"I had breakfast yesterday with Phoebe and Kristen."

The line went silent. Not surprising, given Tasha mentioned his high school sweetheart's name. "Mom's trying to get her phone. Merry Christmas, sis. Love you."

"Love you." Tasha waited for the handoff of the cell phone.

"That boy." Mom muttered a phrase in Russian. "Did you get your white Christmas?"

Tasha pointed her phone at the window for Mom to see. "It's snowing right now."

"Good for you. Phoebe sent me a video of your winter ice show this morning. Why you not mention it?"

Phoebe would do something like that. The woman was always sticking her nose where it didn't belong, but she also did it with kindness. Still… "Phoebe only knew because I needed some costumes."

"I thought I recognized them."

Tasha's jaw dropped. "You watched the show?"

"All of us did."

For once, Tasha didn't hold her breath, didn't tense, didn't cross her fingers. No matter what Mom said, Tasha was proud of the show and especially the performers, including herself.

"The choreography was simpler than you've done for our shows, but you didn't have the same number of skilled skaters, either. You did a fabulous job. And you're skating stronger than when you won bronze."

"Thank you."

"I would have been at your performance if I'd known." The hurt in Mom's voice was unmistakable.

"It was a small-town Christmas show. I didn't think you'd care."

"I care. We all care, but I would have probably tried to turn it into a much bigger production." The hurt tone turned into amused.

"Broadway."

"Off-Broadway given the outdoor rink," Mom teased, letting Tasha know everything was okay. "The only thing I didn't like was your ex-partner. He's a…"

"Tool!" Dad and Alek shouted in the background.

"He is." Tasha would thank Phoebe for sending her mom the video. "You were right, Mom. I'm doing what you suggested. Putting the past behind me so I can move forward. Coming here. Working on the show. Seeing Drew. Performing again. I got the closure I needed. No one will drag me down again."

"I'm happy to hear that. Seattle will be a nice transition spot."

Yelena Ramson spoke as if it were a done deal. Mom never gave up. Neither would Tasha. "It might be."

That was all she would say.

"Hey, Tasha." Dad appeared on the phone. His hair was grayer now, but he was still handsome and in shape. "You've had a rough time, and we should have handled selling the rink differently."

Tasha raised her chin. "Yes, you should have. Finding out the way I did hurt. As much as when you told me not to say anything about what happened with Drew. All to protect Alek's hockey career."

"Back then, I said I could handle whatever happened," Alek spoke up. He tired to get int the picture with Mom and Dad. "There was no reason for Tasha not to speak up."

"It would have to much of a distraction," Mom countered. "No team would have wanted that kind of attention with a young player. It was right decision."

Maybe for her and Dad, but not for Tasha. "Well,

I stood up to Drew at the show and spoke to Savannah yesterday. She admitted he's the reason I was fired from the ice show in November, but he won't be bothering me again."

Alek cursed. "I'll kill him."

"You'll do no such thing." Mom's voice was firm though Dad didn't appear as convinced.

"Mom's right. Drew's not worth a lawsuit or jailtime," Tasha agreed.

"He owes you a huge apology." There was an unfamiliar edge to Alek's voice.

Her brother wasn't wrong. "So do mom and dad."

Mom gasped.

Alek laughed. "Tasha is right. You do. You blindsided both of us by selling the rink."

"You ripped my job away. The rink was the only stability I had in my life."

"I'm sorry," Mom and Dad said at the same time.

"We told you we handled it wrong," Dad added. "One hundred percent we made a mistake."

"We'll make it up to you." Mom didn't hesitate to answer. "Somehow. And it's all worked out. You finally skated in public again. You were breathtaking."

"We're both so proud of you, sweetheart," Dad said. "Watching you skate in the show... I have no words."

"He cried almost as much as Mom!" Alek shouted.

"Nothing wrong with crying," Dad defended

himself. "I know we messed up but the rink, but we're here for you. Always. I love you."

Tasha sniffled. "I love you. Merry Christmas."

"Merry Christmas, tiny skater." Dad had called Tasha that for as long as she remembered.

"We'll call after we've opened your gifts," Mom said. "We have brunch reservations."

"On Christmas morning?"

"It's a big thing here." The words sounded like a shrug. "Love you."

"Love you too." The line disconnected.

Maybe Tasha should pack up this morning and drive to Seattle. She could be there before dinnertime.

Bet Mom would like that. Dad too. Even Alek.

The truth was, Tasha would enjoy it. She needed to check the weather forecast to see if chains were required. But if they weren't…

Her family loved her. Gold or bronze didn't define them.

Well, her mom—sort of.

But Tasha had fixated on it and so much else.

None of them was perfect, especially her. If she accepted her family for who they were, not how she wanted them to be—the same as she wanted from them—their relationship might improve.

It was worth a try.

She returned to opening her bounty of gifts—there had to be at least a dozen—which ranged from flavored candy canes to a scented candle in a jar. Such a thoughtful group of kids and parents.

"The Carol of the Bells" played next.

One present remained—a small square box wrapped in craft paper and tied with twine.

Tasha reached for it. "No tag or card."

Underneath the wrapping paper was a white box. She removed the lid. A folded piece of paper sat on top of the tissue paper. She opened it.

Tasha,

Thanks for all your hard work on the show. It made Christmas for me. The same way your being here made the holiday season extra special. I'm sorry for everything that happened. I take full responsibility. I never meant to hurt you, but I did, and I hope you will forgive me.

I want you to have a keepsake, something to remind you of the Christmas you spent in Berry Lake.

Merry Christmas,

Elias

Tasha reread the note three times. Okay, four, but who was counting?

She folded back the tissue paper to see the top of an ornament. With trembling fingers, she removed it from the box.

"Oh, Elias."

This wasn't a generic ornament. The glass bulb was

like the hand-painted ones she'd seen at Charlene's. Only the image was different.

A woman skated on the lake. She peered closer. "That's me."

Off to the side was a man with a brown and white dog at his feet.

"Elias and Higgins."

He must have asked the artist to paint this for me.

As Tasha cradled the ornament in her hands, tears welled in her eyes. She blinked them away to examine the opposite side of the ornament that showed her and Elias skating on the lake with Higgins watching them from shore.

"Why did he do this?"

The gesture touched her. Elias must have commissioned this before…

But he could have kept the ornament for himself. She cradled it to her chest. The bulb would be a keepsake for Christmases to come, a reminder of Berry Lake, Higgins, and Elias.

She glanced at the box of notecards with books on them from Katie Byrne. One of those would work perfectly for a thank-you card. Tasha could drop it off in his mailbox when she left.

But first, she needed to pack. She stood and made her way across the living room.

A dog barked.

Something scratched at the door.

She opened it.

Higgins barreled inside covered in snow. He wore his sweater and collar but no leash.

"How did you get here?"

He shook, sending snow over the living room.

"Off on another adventure?"

His tail wagged.

"Let me write a thank-you to your dad, and then I'll take you home."

Tasha grabbed a pen from the kitchen and scribbled a thank you. Except the words didn't stop after writing, *thank you.* She wrote from the heart, more than she first intended, and hoped the words were coherent. She put the card in the envelope, put *Elias* on the front, shrugged on her jacket, and shoved the envelope into her pocket.

"I don't have a leash, which means I'll have to carry you."

Higgins panted.

"No, I don't trust you not to make a run for it."

The dog tilted his head.

She slipped on her boots. "Don't play innocent with me."

Carefully, she picked him up and carried him toward Elias's house. A scraping sound filled the air.

Elias shoveled the walkway to his next-door neighbor's house. He wore boots, snow pants, a hat, gloves, and a heavy-duty parka she hadn't seen before.

His cheeks were pink from the cold. Mountain men had never been her type, but he looked as gorgeous as ever.

Do. Not. Go. There.

She couldn't. He'd apologized, but he hadn't asked for a second chance or even to see her again. Besides, weather willing, she wasn't staying in town much longer.

Tasha came closer. "Hey."

"Higgins?" Elias glanced at his house and rubbed the back of his neck with his free hand. "He's supposed to be inside. How did he end up with you?"

"No idea." She appreciated the dog not squirming. Higgins might be small, but he was solid. "I heard scratching at my door. When I opened it, he ran inside the cottage. I didn't want you to worry."

"Thanks. I had no idea he'd gotten out of the house. It must have been when I came outside."

"Do you usually shovel while snow is still falling?"

"No." He half laughed. "My neighbors are retired. Their snowblower broke, and they were worried about the snow getting too deep for a family member who uses a walker. I offered to help."

Of course, he did. That was what nice guys did.

A good thing she held Higgins, or she would have brushed the snow from Elias's shoulders.

"Here…" Elias leaned his shovel against the house. "I've cleared enough for now. I'll take Mister Escape Artist."

She handed over Higgins, fighting the urge to bump her arm against Elias's, if only for some contact. Okay, getting over him wouldn't be easy, but seeing him drove home that realization.

"What am I going to do with you?" He hugged Higgins close to him.

Tasha caught a sigh before it escaped. The two were meant to be together. She hoped he realized how good Higgins was for him before tomorrow. Elias would regret returning the dog to the rescue.

He looked at Tasha. "I'm sorry you had to come out in the snow."

The way the snow surrounded them made her think of being inside a snow globe someone kept shaking.

"No problem." Talk about awkward. She reached into her pocket, pulled out the envelope, and handed it to him. Well, she slipped the note between his left hand and Higgins. "I wanted to drop off a thank-you note for the gift. The ornament will be the perfect keepsake. I'll treasure it forever."

Ugh. Way to pour it on.

This wasn't the first time she'd rambled around him, and the way his gaze held hers made Tasha wish she was the one in his arms.

Elias's smile widened, taking her heart with it. "I hoped you'd like it."

"I do. A lot." More snow settled on his hat and

shoulders. Hers too. "I'm thinking of leaving today. Driving to Seattle to eat dinner with my family."

He stared at her with his lips parted. He didn't even blink. "I thought you were staying until the thirty-first."

"It's Christmas."

"Be careful, I—" His expression tightened for a second before relaxing as if he'd caught himself. "You're not used to driving in snow."

"I'm not, but I have chains." Using her sleeve, she wiped away the snow pelting her face. "Though the weather isn't looking very promising at the moment."

He started to speak but stopped himself. His lips parted again. "You shouldn't spend Christmas alone."

"That's why I came to Berry Lake. Whatever happens, I'll be okay." And Tasha would be. She would make the most of the day whether there or on the road. She scratched behind Higgins's ear. "You two need to get out of the snow, and so do I. Merry Christmas."

"Merry Christmas."

Two simple words. They weren't nearly enough.

The pain in her chest told her it was time to go. But she had one more thing to say to him. So many people had walked away from her without saying goodbye. She wouldn't be like them.

Tasha took a breath, the icy, wet air stinging her lungs. "Goodbye, Elias."

Not waiting for a reply, Tasha walked away. The snow continued falling, faster and harder. She concentrated on her steps to keep from thinking about him. It was more apparent than ever that even though they hadn't known each other long, she would need lots of time to get over him.

Don't look back.

Not that she could see him. She hunched and trudged down the lane.

Her Christmas was not only white but a whiteout.

Be careful what you wish for…

Tasha had to laugh, which was better than wanting to cry, right?

Thirteen

Say something.

Elias should. He opened his mouth, but nothing came out. Words had finally failed him. The only time that had happened before was with Tasha. And now…

He watched her disappear into the snow, falling like a blanket of white. He growled. "What's wrong with me?"

Higgins barked.

"I don't want to hear anything from you. You're a disobedient dog for escaping." Elias headed to the porch, wiped the snow from his boots, and entered the house. As soon as the door latched closed, he placed Higgins on the floor and removed his boots. "Though thanks for bringing Tasha to me."

Even if it had only been for the dog's sake.

Elias removed his outerwear and gloves before he sweated to death.

Tasha's envelope dropped to the floor, and he snatched it up. "How did you sneak out?"

Higgins trotted to the fireplace, where his new pillow waited for him as if he were the king of the castle.

"That's not your throne."

Only a Christmas present from Elias so Higgins wouldn't have to lie on the hardwood when he wanted to warm up by the fire.

"Look at all the stuff you got for Christmas. Santa Paws brought you so many new toys and treats. Why would you run away from home?" Elias kneeled next to Higgins. "You missed Tasha, didn't you?"

Higgins didn't disagree.

"I get it." Elias patted the dog's head. "But please don't do that again. I can't lose you too."

Higgins stared at Elias.

"What?"

Higgins tilted his head.

Elias remembered what was in his hand. He opened the envelope, removed the card, and read.

Elias,

Merry Christmas! Thank you for the gorgeous ornament. What a unique way to remember Berry Lake. You and Higgins too. I appreciate your apology and forgive you. Neither of us is a pro when expressing our needs and talking about what we're feeling. I'm so happy we met. You've helped me grow in so many ways. I closed the door to my past and am ready to move forward finally. I'll always be grateful to you for that.

Take care,
Tasha

P.S. You and Higgins belong together. Just saying.

Elias laughed. He reread the note and wiped his wet eyes. So much to think about, but one thing was clear.

"She's right, you know." He touched Higgins. The fur against Elias's palm had become as natural as waking up in bed with the dog at his feet. "You belong with me. Or me with you. Either way, this works."

Higgins leaned into Elias's hand.

"Besides…" He rubbed the dog. "It'll be easier not having to move all your old stuff, plus all the new stuff, to the rescue."

Higgins's tail wagged.

"Want to make me a foster failure?"

As if on cue, Higgins barked.

"But I'm not wearing the T-shirt."

Higgins panted.

That was settled, but Tasha…

A million and one thoughts pummeled Elias's brain, but one rose above the others.

"I don't want to lose her, either." Elias waved her notecard. "This is evidence, Higgins. Proof things aren't over yet."

A plan finally formed. He put the odds of it working at twenty-five percent, but he had nothing to lose.

Except for the best thing in his life.

No offense to Higgins, who was the second-best thing.

Elias grabbed his cell phone and typed a text.

Me: *Merry Christmas. Is there room for one more?*
Grammy: *Other than Higgins?*
Me: *Yes.*
Grammy: *Of course, dear.*
Me: *I don't know if she'll come.*
Grammy: *I'll have a place setting ready for Tasha.*
Me: *I didn't say it was her.*
Grammy: *Am I correct?*
Me: *Yes.*
Grammy: *There's been talk.*
Me: *I'm not sure if things will work out.*
Grammy: *I listened to Selena Tremblay's podcast. What does she call herself?*
Me: *Selena T.*
Grammy: *I remember now. She said to follow your heart. Do that, and you'll have no regrets.*
Me: *Thanks. I will. I love you.*
Grammy: *Right back at you, kid.*

"Step one accomplished." Elias patted Higgins. "Stay here and warm up."

Elias put on his outerwear and boots and stepped outside into the snowstorm. No doubt his shoveling efforts had been for naught, but he'd tried.

The wind blew. Snowflakes hit his skin like icy daggers. His clothes and gloves kept the rest of him toasty warm. He focused on his steps. Each one brought him closer to Tasha. Pinewood Lane wasn't long, but he was happy when he reached the last cottage.

He wasn't sure what he wanted to say. Berry Lake was his hometown. It had been the place where he grew up and now lived. He'd been given everything and never had to stand up for himself. Oh, sure he'd done it for clients like Missy Hanford, but never himself until recently. But he'd realized something else. His job wasn't the reason he'd been feeling stuck. It was his life. He'd made the decision to work so much. He'd let his job dictate everything. And that was on him. But meeting Tasha and Higgins had shown him how much was missing in his life. The two made Berry Lake feel like home in a way nothing had before. Elias didn't want to lose that feeling, lose them. He would stand up for what he wanted, for them, and do whatever it took.

On the porch, he brushed the snow from his shoulders. His finger hovered in front of the doorbell. His long exhale floated in the air. "Follow your heart."

Elias jabbed the button.

The door opened. Tasha stood wearing socks, holding a steaming mug, and a shocked expression. She froze until she ushered him inside.

Tasha closed the door. "Is everything okay? Higgins?"

The words he wanted to say got stuck in his throat again.

Follow your heart.

"Higgins is fine. I'm not." There, Elias had said it. Not everything, but that was a start. "I hate how things happened between us. I made a mistake, and you forgave me. So, I'm standing here, dripping snow on the floor, wanting to know if you'll give me a second chance."

He ran through the mental list in his head. That covered what he wanted to say. Except…

"I don't know about you, but I'm not ready for whatever's between us to end."

She bit her lip. "Would you like a cup of coffee?"

Elias hadn't known what she would say, but he hadn't expected her to offer him a warm beverage. "Sure."

As "All I Want For Christmas Is You" by Mariah Carey played, he pulled off his gloves and boots. Next, he removed his hat and jacket. If she asked him to leave, he would have an extra minute or two to plead his case while he put on his outerwear.

Colorful gas flames danced in the fireplace. The tree was lit up in the corner. Very Christmassy.

He did a double take. The ornament he'd given her hung front and center.

I have a shot.

Prepared to aim, he sat on the couch and rubbed his palms over his pants.

Tasha placed two mugs on the table and sat on the opposite end of the couch. A cushion separated them. "I…"

"Look…" he said at the same time.

Her gaze met his. The tension between them was palpable.

Elias picked up the coffee closest to him. The cup warmed his cold hands. "You can go first."

She angled her shoulders toward him. "I'm surprised to see you, but I'm happy you're here."

He released the breath he'd been holding and set the coffee on the table. "Me too. I wanted to stop you earlier, but I didn't know what to say. You nailed it in the note about me not saying what I'm feeling or what I want."

"I struggle with that too. It's hard."

"Losing you would be harder."

Tasha inhaled sharply. "You…"

"I own up to screwing up the first time, and I want a second chance."

"I'd like that too." She glanced into her coffee before meeting his gaze.

Her eyes were warm and thoughtful. It was all he could do not to hug her.

"I didn't want to say goodbye earlier," she continued. "But I didn't know what else to say. Everything came to a head when I saw Drew. It was years of not speaking up. Things built inside me, as I tried to ignore what had happened with him, my parents, even my friend, Kristen. You got the brunt of everything. I'm sorry."

"You have no reason to apologize. I didn't do my due diligence. But we both need to communicate better."

She reached across the space between them and held his hand. "I agree. We need to talk about what's going on with us even if it's hard."

He nodded. "I want this to work."

"Same."

Elias scooted closer. "I'd like to spend the rest of Christmas with you. Will you come with Higgins and me to my grandparents' house?"

"Today?"

"Now."

She laughed. "Well, I didn't want to be alone on Christmas, so that sounds great. Only I don't have presents for anyone."

"Neither does Higgins."

She laughed. "Okay, then. I need to change clothes. Casual?"

"Casual and Christmassy if you have anything."

"Give me a second."

"You can have sixty."

"Generous."

"That's one hundred percent because of you."

"We can share." She stood.

Elias pulled out his phone and sent a text.

Me: *Expert advice. It worked.*

Grammy: *Excellent. I've set a place for Tasha and your grandfather's hanging extra mistletoe.*

Elias laughed. Extra mistletoe sounded perfect.

"I'm ready." Tasha came out in black pants, a red sweater, and a poinsettia scarf around her neck. "A skater from the show gave me the scarf. Will this outfit do?"

His breath caught in his throat. She was stunning.

Her smile filled him with joy. "I take it that's a yes."

Not trusting his voice, Elias moved over to her.

Forget the mistletoe. They had their own kind of Christmas magic right there. He went closer—a man on a mission. "You're gorgeous."

She opened her mouth, and he kissed her. A kiss full of warmth and possibilities. She returned his kiss, running her fingers through his hair.

Best Christmas ever?

Yeah. At least until next year.

Fourteen

On the fifth day of Christmas, December twenty-ninth, Tasha didn't think she would receive one gold ring, let alone five, but she imagined one on her left ring finger anyway. Not today, but in the future.

Joy overflowed inside her. Was it too soon to be thinking so far ahead?

Maybe, but when all her dreams were coming true in ways she never imagined, she allowed herself the indulgence. Christmas with Elias's family had been wonderful. As soon as they'd walked through the door, Grammy had maneuvered them under the mistletoe to the delight of Elias's grandfather and dad. The holiday hadn't been the same as if she'd been with her family, but that was fine. She'd enjoyed having a Carpenter Christmas.

Unfortunately, her time in Berry Lake was running out. Tasha had one more Christmas wish—she wished time would freeze like the top layer of Berry Lake.

Silly, yes. But…

A sideward glance showed her Elias sitting next to her on an old fallen log with Higgins at his feet.

Her pulse kicked up a notch as if in the warm-up phase. A typical—and welcome—reaction around Elias. Forever with them sounded awesome. If only…

Tasha sighed. Her long exhale hung on the chilly air like a fluffy cloud. The only thing missing? Blue skies, but she didn't mind winter's overcast gray. She pictured a sunny, bluebird day. Funnily enough, she didn't see the ocean in her daydream.

Elias laced his ice skates. "You look deep in thought."

"Just thinking."

"About?"

Neither was good at sharing their feelings until pushed to the brink, but both were trying to do better. "How wonderful being here is. I'm not ready to stop celebrating the twelve days of Christmas."

He touched her arm, a soft gesture that reaffirmed their connection and his being by her side, no matter what.

"You don't have to." Elias squeezed. "There are still seven days to go."

Except they wouldn't be together for those.

Tasha's shoulders sagged but only for an instant. Nothing would ruin her remaining time there. She wouldn't let it. "I heard from the cottage's owner. You were right about a new owner. He takes possession on January first, so I can't extend my stay beyond the thirty-first. I should get back to Wishing Bay, anyway."

As soon as the words were out, she regretted saying them. That was fear talking. With the rink closed, she didn't have to be anywhere.

"If that's what you want to do, fine. A few hours apart won't change the way I feel about you." Elias cupped the side of her face with his gloved hand. "But I have two spare bedrooms. You're welcome to either."

Staying with him seemed a logical choice. "Thanks, but I don't want to mess anything up."

Elias laughed, and she dreamed of growing old, hearing his laughter day and night. He tapped the tip of her nose. "I don't care if you're a slob."

He always made her smile, and one spread across her face, warming her from the inside. How had she gotten so lucky?

She sent a wave of gratitude to Higgins for making sure they'd met. "I didn't mean a literal mess. I meant you and me."

"We're fine." He brushed his lips over hers. "But I want you to be comfortable. You give so much. I don't want you to do anything because you think I want it."

"I won't. I can't. That's what I did before." With her family, Drew, Kristen. "I've learned my lesson. Thanks for helping me learn that lesson."

"You helped me, too."

Which was how it should be. Everything about him…them. "Things are so good right now. I'm happier than I've been."

He leaned his shoulder into hers. "And they'll keep being good. And we'll keep being happy. I'm one to talk but relax."

His confidence soothed her. Still, she half laughed. "I don't think *relax* is in my vocabulary."

"Something for us to both work on because it wasn't in mine until I met you."

Her heart bumped. "I love the sound of us."

"Same." Elias extended his arm. "Let's skate before we get too cold."

Higgins, his leash secured to the log, sat patiently watching them.

She owed that no-longer-a-foster dog so much. "Higgins likes it out here."

"He wants to be wherever we are, though I hadn't planned for him to want to sleep with me each night. I thought once he got adjusted to the house, that would end."

Joy overflowed. "You've gone totally dog dad."

Heat pooled in his cheeks. "What can I say? But I now get the actual meaning of animal rescue. Higgins has given me so much more than I've given him."

"You rescued each other." *And both of you rescued me.* "You were destined to be a foster failure."

Elias glanced over his shoulder at Higgins. "Sabine gave me a *foster failure* T-shirt when I signed the adoption papers."

"She probably ordered one in your size before she dropped off Higgins." Tasha stepped onto the ice. "The two of you are a perfect match."

He followed her. "You, Higgins, and I are the perfect match."

"Isn't that what I said?" she joked.

Their skate blades carved into the ice—her second favorite sound. First was Elias, whether it was his voice or his laugh.

As she glided across the lake, The cold air hit her face. Skating had always been where she felt free to express herself. But standing in front of an audience waiting for the music to begin had turned into an internal battle. Anticipation could make a performance go either way, but she'd found new confidence—a new her. She believed she could not only skate but do anything she wanted without fear, fear of dealing with Drew's jealousy and wrath or Mom's criticism. Elias and the town of Berry Lake had helped her rediscover herself and her joy of skating. Oh, Higgins too. She couldn't forget him.

After a few laps on their own, snow fell from the sky—a perfect accent to an already spectacular day.

Elias skated up to her. "Stop for a minute."

She did, tilting her head back to catch a snowflake on her tongue.

He held her hand. "There's another reason I couldn't return Higgins."

"What's that?" she asked, staring at him.

"He's the reason I met you."

Her heart stumbled, but in a good way. She knew whatever happened, Elias was there to catch her or help her put the pieces together again. "I'm so happy I tripped over his leash that day. This has been the best Christmas ever."

He took a breath and another and gazed into her eyes.

She recognized that pensive gleam. "What?"

"Stay in Berry Lake with Higgins and me. There's no rink back in Wishing Bay."

Chills—the good kind having nothing to do with the cold temperature—raced through Tasha. She forced herself to breathe. "I want to stay. But the park's rink goes away after the New Year."

"There's another one thirty minutes away. That's closer than Wishing Bay, and Logan Tremblay's planning to build one in Berry Lake, so he can skate closer to home."

Like Mom and Dad.

"There's another option." Elias squeezed her hands. "I gave myself until January to decide what to do about my job. Having you here has made it better. Higgins too. I'm working less, enjoying life more. But you're the most important thing to me. If there's another place you'd rather be, Wishing Bay or a larger city, that's fine by me. As long as we're together."

She couldn't believe what he was saying. "Your job and family…"

"I want you to be my family, too. I know I might be rushing things."

"I don't mind rushing."

"Good because I'm not patient when it comes to you." He brushed his lips over hers. "You and Higgins are the two most important things in my life. I can find another job. We can visit Berry Lake."

Her heart slammed against her rib cage. No one had ever been willing to sacrifice for her. Not like this. But Elias…

"I love you." *Guess we're still traveling at light speed.* But Tasha couldn't stop herself from saying the three words. She didn't want to. "I love you so much."

His eyes widened. So did his smile. "I love you too."

Every nerve ending tingled. So much adrenaline pounded through her veins. She might land a quad if she tried. "I want us to be together."

"This year is only our first Christmas together. The first of a lifetime together."

He let go of her hands, dropped onto one knee, and pulled something out of his pocket.

A ring. A diamond solitaire in a shiny gold setting.

She gasped. Her hand covered her mouth.

"This is fast, and I wasn't sure if I should wait, but I wanted to be ready if the opportunity presented itself. It has, and I don't care if a month ago, we didn't know each other. We do now." Affection laced each of his words. "You're the best thing in my life. I want you to know how I feel. How committed I am to you. To us. Tasha Ramson. Will you do me the honor of being my wife?"

Her breath hitched. Warm tears—happy ones— blurred her vision and slipped down her cheeks.

"Yes." Tasha thought she might be dreaming. Elias was everything she hadn't known she needed, wanted, loved. "Yes, I'll marry you."

He removed her glove and placed the ring on her finger.

Tasha stared at the gorgeous diamond and giggled. She got a gold ring, after all.

He wiped her face. "Thank you. We don't have to rush the wedding, but this way you know I'm committed to you."

"And I'm committed to you." Wholeheartedly.

They kissed.

More snow fell.

That was when it hit her. Her lips parted. "The way we are right now is like one side of the ornament you gave me."

"It is." He laughed. "Hope asked how we met, but I told her I didn't want her painting you on the ice with

Higgins on top of you. She must've come up with this scene herself."

Tasha would have to ask her. "I suggest we start a new tradition. Each year, we ask Hope to paint us an ornament. She can paint something that happened over the year."

"I'd love that."

A bark sounded.

"Sounds like Higgins agrees." She glanced at the dog, who sat staring at them.

"Of course, he does." Elias helped her put her glove on. "Higgins is a smart dog. He found you, didn't he?"

"He did. And I'll be forever grateful." Tasha kissed Elias. A kiss full of hopes, of dreams, and of a future together.

Epilogue

From *Skating Spins & Turns*:

Pairs skating champions Savannah Savory and Drew Maddox have postponed their wedding until after the Winter Games. Savoy said she wanted no distractions from their skating.

The skating world has been abuzz after watching Tasha Ramson's sweet Christmas ice show and her breathtaking finale number. The skater proved she has the "it" factor. She will be performing in a benefit ice show, and we can't wait to see her perform again. It's been too long.

We'd also like to congratulate Tasha and her fiancé, Elias Carpenter, on their engagement. She is also officially becoming a choreographer. Not only are we here for it, but so are skaters. We've heard there's already a waitlist for her services. She will be based in Berry Lake, Washington, where a state-of-the-art skating facility will be built this spring.

* * * * *

Thanks for reading *The Last Cottage on Pinewood Lane*. If you enjoyed Tasha and Elias's story, check out *Cupcakes & Crumbs*, the first book in the Berry Lake Cupcake Posse series. Elias is introduced in book two of the series. I hope to release the Wishing Bay series in 2023. The first book features Kristen and Alek.

Join Melissa's newsletter to receive a FREE story
and hear about upcoming and new releases,
sales, freebies, and giveaways. Just go to
melissamcclone.com/NLsignup.

I appreciate your help spreading the word. Tell a friend who loves sweet romance about this book and leave a review on your favorite book site. Reviews help readers find books!

Thanks so much!

About the Author

USA Today bestselling author Melissa McClone has written over fifty sweet contemporary romance and women's fiction novels. She lives in the Pacific Northwest with her husband. She has three young adult children, a spoiled Norwegian Elkhound, and cats who think they rule the house. They do!

If you'd like to find Melissa online:
www.melissamcclone.com
www.facebook.com/melissamcclonebooks
www.facebook.com/groups/McCloneTroopers
www.patreon.com/melissamcclone

Other Books by Melissa McClone

The Beach Brides/Indigo Bay Miniseries
Prequels to the Berry Lake Cupcake Posse series…
Jenny (Jenny and Dare)
Sweet Holiday Wishes (Lizzy and Mitch)
Sweet Beginnings (Hope and Josh)
Sweet Do-Over (Marley and Von)
Sweet Yuletide (Sheridan and Michael)
Indigo Bay Sweet Romance Collection (Box Set of all five books)

The Berry Lake Cupcake Posse Series
Can five friends save their small town's beloved bakery?
Cupcakes & Crumbs
Tiaras & Teacups
Kittens & Kisses

Silver Falls Series
The Andrews siblings find love in a
small town in Washington state.
The Christmas Window
A Slice of Summer
A Cup of Autumn

One Night to Forever Series
Can one night change your life…and your relationship status?
Fiancé for the Night
The Wedding Lullaby
A Little Bit Engaged
Love on the Slopes
The One Night To Forever Box Set: Books 1-4

Her Royal Duty
Royal romances with charming princes and dreamy castles...
The Reluctant Princess
The Not-So-Proper Princess
The Proper Princess

The Billionaires of Silicon Forest
Who will be the last single man standing?
The Wife Finder
The Wish Maker
The Deal Breaker
The Gold Digger
The Kiss Catcher
The Game Changer
The Bet Makers (Newsletter exclusive)
The Billionaires of Silicon Forest Prequels
The Billionaires of Silicon Forest Series

Mountain Rescue Series
Finding love in Hood Hamlet
with a little help from Christmas magic…
His Christmas Wish
Her Christmas Secret
Her Christmas Kiss
His Second Chance
His Christmas Family

Quinn Valley Ranch
Two books featuring siblings in a multi-author series...
Carter's Cowgirl
Summer Serenade
Quinn Valley Ranch Two Book Set

A Keeper at Heart Series
These men know what they want, and love isn't on their list.
But what happens when each meets a keeper?
The Groom
The Soccer Star
The Boss
The Husband
The Date
The Tycoon

For the complete list of books, go to melissamcclone.com/books